THE GIRL WHO BLEW UP THE WORLD

A JIMMY RILEY NOIR MYSTERY NOVEL, BOOK 5

MICHAEL LISTER

PULPWOOD PRESS

Ppaperback ISBN: 978-1-947606-14-2

Sign up for Michael's newsletter by clicking here or go to www.MichaelLister.com and receive a free book.

(John Jordan Novels)
Power in the Blood
Blood of the Lamb
Flesh and Blood
(Special Introduction by Margaret Coel)
The Body and the Blood
Blood Sacrifice
Rivers to Blood
Innocent Blood
(Special Introduction by Michael Connelly)
Blood Money
Blood Moon
Blood Cries
Blood Oath
Blood Work
Cold Blood

(Jimmy Riley Novels)
The Girl Who Said Goodbye
The Girl in the Grave
The Girl at the End of the Long Dark Night
The Girl Who Cried Blood Tears
The Girl Who Blew Up the World

In a Spider's Web (short story)
The Big Book of Noir

(Merrick McKnight / Reggie Summers Novels)
Thunder Beach
A Certain Retribution

(Remington James Novels)
Double Exposure
(includes intro by Michael Connelly)
Separation Anxiety

(Sam Michaels / Daniel Davis Novels)
Burnt Offerings
Separation Anxiety

(Love Stories)
Carrie's Gift

(Short Story Collections)
North Florida Noir
Florida Heat Wave
Delta Blues
Another Quiet Night in Desparation

(The Meaning Series)
Meaning Every Moment
The Meaning of Life in Movies

Sign up for Michael's newsletter by clicking here or go to
www.MichaelLister.com and receive a free book.

1

I didn't like what I was doing.

    I was following a woman who reminded me of Lauren for a man who reminded me of me.

Downtown was dark beneath a cloud-shrouded sky, the air thick with the threat of night rain.

It was early January 1944, and unseasonably warm even for North Florida, as if the incoming rain was part of something equatorial.

The woman in question, Rita Welles, was supposed to be at the Ritz Theater with her neighbor and coworker at the phone company, Betty Blackmon, watching Gary Cooper and Ingrid Bergman in Technicolor for the fourth time. Instead, she was walking down Grace Avenue the way women do when they're meeting someone.

Like the best lies, her cover story of seeing *For Whom the Bell Tolls* with Betty was partially true. She had started there. She had even watched some of the picture, but before Cooper could fall for Bergman, she had ducked out the side door and down 4th Street toward a place that was haunted for me.

Nick's was a dark, out-of-the-way bar that served hard liquor for serious drinkers. It had a Wurlitzer jukebox, a small dance floor, and a couple of pool tables in the back, but what it mostly had was hard liquor and plenty of it.

This is where Ruth Ann Johnson, the Salvation Army nurse who had lost her leg helping wounded soldiers in the South Pacific and her life helping me hunt for who killed Lauren, and I used to meet to talk and drink. It was also the place I had tailed Angel Adams to—and where a short middle-aged man fighting over her had put a round into the mirror behind the bar.

As Rita entered the joint, she looked lost.

Seemingly unsure what to do, she began making her way around the fringes of the place, some part of her always pressed up against the wall.

I eased onto a stool at the bar, ordered a bourbon, and watched in the huge mirror behind the bar as Rita move awkwardly around the room.

I had a good view—and not just of Rita, but the entire place—even with the various bottles lined up in front of the mirror and the spider web etched in it above them.

It was the usual raucous crowd. Wainwright Shipyard workers with money to drink, and boys who could die soon and didn't want to think about it.

The USO Club a couple of streets over, where Lauren was working right now, had been created to keep servicemen out of places like this. It just didn't always work.

There were far more men than women—an equation that more often than not added up to big trouble.

"Hiya, Soldier. Buy me a drink?"

I turned to see Betsy Dobbins, Panama City's hardest-working working girl on the stool next to me.

"Hiya Betsy."

"It's Elizabeth tonight," she said.

Betsy—Elizabeth tonight—had had a lot of competition since

the beginning of the war. Working women were everywhere these days—and not just in the factories and shipyards. Unlike Betsy, who was a pro before the war began and would still be long after they called the whole thing off, amateurs flooded the market —"victory girls," "good-time charlottes," and "patriotutes"—many of whom charged little more than a Coke or ice cream sundae.

"Beg your pardon, Elizabeth," I said. "Buy you a drink?"

"Sure, soldier. I'll drink all your hard-earned divorce work."

"Actually it's my wife's inheritance," I said. "She's loaded, so I don't do too much divorce work anymore."

"And she wouldn't object to you buying me a drink?"

"She'd insist."

"Sounds like quite a catch you got yourself there."

I nodded, and returned my attention to the mirror.

Rita was looking for someone. Little doubt about that. And she was going about it in such a conspicuous way that whoever it was couldn't help but see her.

"Pretty girl," Betsy said. "Would your wife insist you watch her too?"

"Actually she does. She chose the case and is footin' the bill. She's convinced the little lady isn't stepping out on her little mister."

"Whatta you think?"

"Clearly she's steppin' out," I said.

"Tell me more about this wife of yours," she said. "She sounds too good to be true."

"She's too good not to be," I said.

"That sounds almost religious."

"It kinda is."

"Geez fella."

"I know. Sorry. But . . . can't help myself. You knew what we'd been through to be together, you'd understand. And the truth is I just came from seeing Bergman and Cooper. And a joint like this makes me maudlin—especially following a woman like that and sitting next to one like you."

"What's that supposed to mean?"

"Meant it as a compliment," I said. "Thing is, I'm feeling guilty and ashamed too."

"Why's that?"

"Of who I used to be, of who I thought my wife was back then —back when I was following her like I'm following this girl."

I nodded at Rita's reflection in the mirror behind the bar.

"Oh."

"Yeah."

I could see in the mirror that Rita had found someone—just not who she was looking for.

In the back room, between the wall and the farthest pool table, a thick, dark-complected man with a sweaty neck showing out of an open collar was pawing at her like he'd never seen a pretty girl before.

"Looks like your doll needs some help," she said.

I nodded.

"Not that you'd be much with just the one arm. He looks plenty big and strong. And kinda mean."

I watched for a moment longer, hoping someone else would intervene—perhaps the poor sap she was supposed to be meeting. Hated to blow my cover if I didn't have to. But when no one stepped up, I spun around on my barstool and stood.

"Wish me luck," I said to Betsy.

"You're gonna need it."

I started toward the back room, but was still close enough to hear her say, "Even money he rips your other arm off and clubs you to death with it."

2

Emboldened by Betsy's belief in me, I weaved my way through the couples dancing and emerged on the other side more or less unscathed.

"Rita," I said in a loud voice over the music. "What are you doing back here, honey? I told you to meet me at the bar. Come on, we've got to go. We're late to meet Steve and your sister."

She looked confused, but not nearly as much as Sweaty Neck or his pals.

The men scattered around the back room were what you'd expect. Like him, they were redneck ruffians with a few drinks in them. Part of the reason they were here was to fight. They'd have his back in a brawl.

"Beat it, pal. The lady and I are about to dance."

"That's no lady," I said. "That's my wife."

"Finders keepers, little—"

He stopped talking when he caught sight of my missing right.

"Gee, soldier, I'm sorry. I had no idea you were—"

"He ain't no soldier," another man said from the shadows. "He's just a cheap peeper."

"I prefer *affordable private eye*," I said.

"You crackin' wise with me, pal? Pretending you a soldier. I oughta rip the other'n off and give you a good goddamn thrashin' with it."

"The prescient prostitute at the bar put down even money on you doing that very thing, but if we could go back for just a moment. How exactly did I pretend to be a soldier? I'm not pretending to be short a limb either. It's on the level."

"We're gonna enjoy kickin' your teeth in, ain't we boys? I mean more than usual."

"That a usual source of entertainment for you fellas, is it?"

As I had been talking, I had been making eyes and head gestures at Rita, and evidently a few had finally gotten through, because with Sweaty Neck savoring the frivolity his boots and my teeth were about to have, she was able to slip away, slinking back along the wall the way she had come in and out the door without him ever noticing. Not that he would have cared much at this point anyway. His one appetite had overtaken his other.

I began to back away, leading the men out of the poolroom and onto the dance floor. I had wanted to see how many would actually pursue. Four followed me.

"I was hoping it would be fewer," I said, but it was lost in the song on the jukebox and the noise of the crowd.

Now it was time to decide what to do. If I drew my gun, I'd have to use it. Something I didn't want to do. The risk was too great I'd wing one of the dancers. Or worse. Without the gat, I was no match for any one of the men, let alone all four. It occurred to me I could offer to buy them a drink—a not injudicious use of Lauren's money, and one I was certain she would wholeheartedly approve of.

"Whatta you say I buy you fellas a drink?" I said. "Hell, a couple of 'em."

"Whatta you say we mop up the dance floor with you, then take your milk money and buy our own drinks."

That milk money crack meant this sweaty neck bastard was a

proud bully.

"Technically, I'd still be buying them," I said. "Or my wife would."

"Oh, we'll get to your wife," he said. "Just give us time."

They didn't even know Lauren and that still made me mad as hell.

I was still trying to figure my next move when I backed into a wall and had to stop.

But something wasn't right. I was now only in the middle of the dance floor—a place I was fairly certain they hadn't put a wall since I had crossed the floor just a few minutes before.

"Nothin' in this world I hate so much as a bully," the wall said.

"I recognize that voice," I said.

I glanced back and up to see Orson Ferrell, one of my oldest and best friends from school.

"Orca?" I said. "Is that you?"

"It's me, Jimmy my boy. Whatta we mixed up in this time?"

Before I could respond, Sweaty Neck rushed us—a move I assumed meant it'd be quicker to show rather than explain to Orc what was going on.

With one fluid motion, Orca reached over and past me and brought his hammer of a hand down in a fist that bopped Sweaty Neck on the top of the head like a field mouse.

The thick, sweaty, mean man crumpled to the dance floor, his huddled heap now being danced around.

Suddenly, as if remembering they were in the middle of an important match, the other men turned and all but ran into the back room.

"I've always found most people can be reasoned with," Orca said. "Haven't you?"

"Can't imagine I've found it to quite the extent you have, big fella, but I certainly see what you mean."

"By God but it's good to see you, Jimmy," Orca said. "You're just the person I been lookin' for. I need your help."

3

It was funny to see Orson without Ernie. They had always gone together like Moby and Ahab.

The three of us had been the best of buddies growing up, often referred to by those around us as the Three Musketeers, but the truth was, Orson and Ernie were closer to each other than I was to either one of them. I was always odd man out, even if only slightly so—a dynamic that had increased with the war. They got to serve; I did not.

"Where you been keepin' yourself, pal?" Orson said. "It's been too long."

We had largely lost touch—something that had far more to do with my shame and embarrassment at not being in the trenches with them than the trenches themselves.

"My life is boring," I said.

"Ain't what I hear, pal. Don't be so modest."

"Tell me about yours, the war. What're you doing home? Doesn't look like you're missing any parts."

"Didn't leave any parts over there, but brought a few extras home with me. Shrapnel in my leg and a metal plate in my head.

Let's grab a beer and head outside. This screwy music has the plate in my head vibrating—and not in no kinda good way."

I grabbed a couple of beers and we walked outside, Sweaty Neck still sleeping as dead hoofers trembled around him.

It took some effort, but we found a nice quiet place down a little ways on 4th near a dark warehouse.

"Was it as bad as everybody says?" I said.

"Worse."

I nodded and frowned, a fresh wave of guilt washing over me.

"I believed in God before I went over there," he said. "Now I only believe in hell."

I wasn't sure what to say to that, so I said nothing, and we fell quiet a moment.

I thought about how different our experiences over the past few years had been. We had both been through hell of a sorts, but Lauren had made me believe in God, in love, in spite of hell, while for Orson there had only been hell.

"God, but it's good to be back," he said.

"Really great to have you back," I said, awkwardly patting him on the back with my left hand.

I felt bad for him and wanted to express some kind of sympathy, of solidarity in the hell he was in—and for as awkward as the past was, it seemed to achieve the desired effect.

He looked at me, our eyes locking, nodded, and began to smile.

"How about Ernie?" I said. "Where is he? How is he doing?"

"Be home soon. Convalescing in a hospital over there. Lost an eye and two fingers."

"Sorry to hear that," I said.

"That's what I need your help with," he said. "It's what I'm doin' in this hell hole tonight."

"What's that?"

"Lookin' for Ernie's girl," he said. "She's missing. He asked me to look her up and keep an eye on her until he got home, and I can't even do that right."

"We'll find her, don't you worry."

Betsy and an eager john, who she'd managed to hook before he drank all his money, walked out of Nicks, strolled past us, and disappeared into the darkness on the other side of the warehouse.

Orson had raised his eyebrows at her, then stared after her until she couldn't be seen anymore, and I wondered how long it had been since he had been with a woman.

"She was his girl before we left," Orson was saying. "You remember Joan, don't you? They're mad about each other. Were gonna marry. She really, really wanted to. They both did, but he didn't want her to be tied down while he was away, wanted to make sure he was gonna come home. Now he's comin' home and she ain't here."

I didn't remember a lot about Joan—never knew her very well. I only remembered thinking back then that Ernie Ford and Joan Wynn were perfect for one another.

"How long's she been missing? Where was she last seen? Who have you talked to? What do they know?"

"Jimmy Riley is on the case," he said.

"When does Ernie get back? How long do we have? Have you told him?"

"Any day now," he said. "Don't know exactly. Have I told him? Are you kidding? You think I want to write something like that in a letter to a guy lying there thinking only of her?"

I looked at my watch.

"I've got to get over and pick up Lauren at the—"

"Lauren, that your girl?"

I nodded. "She volunteers at the USO. I've got to—"

"Joan worked at the USO. It's one of the last places she was seen. I think maybe she ran into the wrong fella there and . . ."

"You wanna go with me to talk to her or meet me in my office in the morning to—"

"Ain't stopping 'til I find her. I'm coming."

4

"I remember Joan," Lauren said. "I didn't realize she was missing. Figured her fella had come home. She said he was going to soon."

Lauren was as beautiful as ever, but looked tired and frail. She was overdoing it, but wouldn't hear of doing any less than she was —and often talked of doing more.

She no longer wore her hair to hide her burns, and I hoped it was because I had convinced her just how truly beautiful she was in spite of them, but suspected it was at least in part due to the fact that every other person you passed these days was marred in some way.

We were standing out in front of the USO near the end of Harrison, after I had introduced Lauren and Orson and told her about Joan and Ernie.

Rain was imminent, the moist night pregnant with it, and the increasingly brisk breeze blew the American and USO flags to the right of the building, whipping and snapping the cloth about and clanging the rigging against the flagpole.

"Before we go on, can I just ask . . . Did Rita meet anyone?"

I shook my head. "She did not."

Lauren smiled her brilliant, sweet smile that said people were better than I thought and so was the world.

"She got stood up," I said. "And in a dangerous place too."

As usual the USO was hopping. People coming and going, milling about—on the large front porch, in the front yard, and in the back down by the bay. Music, talking, laughter, as well as dancing feet on the hardwood floors could be heard from inside, its volume spiking every time the door opened.

We had stepped several feet away near our car.

"What do you remember about Joan?" I asked.

"She was a sweet, kind girl. Spent hours listening to the frightened young soldiers cycling through here."

"But no funny business, right?" Orson said.

Lauren shot a look at me and said, "No. No funny business."

She wasn't sure how much she could say in front of Orson, and I appreciated her discretion.

"Anybody get fresh with her?" Orson said. "Try anything?"

"Sure, but no more than normal."

I was reminded of what I tried not to think about—how many lonely young men were falling for Lauren each night, how many making a play for the woman who meant the world to me, the entire world.

"Any regulars?" I asked. "Any guy in particular have a hard time hearing 'no'?"

She shot me another look.

"I'll have to think about it."

"Was she acting strange in the days leading up to her disappearance? Did anything happen?"

Again the look.

"Tell you what," I said to Orca. "Lauren's exhausted and in poor health to begin with. Let me get her home. I'll talk to her in the morning. Meet me at my office around eight."

"Make it nine," Lauren said.

"Nine," I said. "It's a walkup on Harrison not far from the Ritz Theater. Easy to find."

"Thanks, Jimmy," he said. "You're a real pal."

"Get some sleep tonight," I said. "We'll find her. And before Ernie gets home—so she can welcome him herself. Okay?"

5

"Wasn't sure what I could say in front of Orson," Lauren said as we drove away.

"You did good. He may find out everything eventually anyway, but . . . better to see what we're dealing with first."

We drove through the late night traffic of downtown, careful to keep an eye on the myriad pedestrians—many of whom were attempting to walk without the aid of sobriety.

Since the start of the war, Harrison Avenue had stopped sleeping. Twenty-four hours a day people spilled out of the stores and restaurants, hung over balconies, congregated on the sidewalks and sometimes into the streets, and entered and exited hotels and drugstores and buses.

It was every bit as busy at night as it was during the day—maybe more so.

"You mind if we swing by Gary and Rita's on our way home?" Lauren said.

"Was gonna ask if you felt up for it."

"I do."

"So tell me about Joan. And don't hold anything back."

"I'm not saying she was doing anything she wasn't supposed to," she said, "but . . . I wouldn't've said she was in a relationship. She seemed restless, like she was looking, you know? Nothing very overt. She was subtle. But like I say it surprised me to hear she was in a relationship. You okay to talk about this?"

I'd had a hard time with Lauren working in the USO, spending so much time with single young men under such intense and extreme conditions, but I knew it was something she had to do, a way to give back, a way to help win the war—one of many she was doing.

I nodded.

We eased past the Ford dealership, the Texaco station, and the Tennessee House.

"Our job in there is to help the soldiers focus on what they're fighting for, to help them relax and leave some of the pressure they carry around with them at the door. Lots of ways to do that. Best way is to get them to talk. I get them to tell me about their hometown, their family, their friends, and their girl back home. I don't talk a lot, mostly just listen. When I do talk, I always talk about you, about us. Gently remind them I'm taken as taken can be, but also let them know what's possible, what they can have with their girl if they don't trade it away for something unworthy of them, and if we win the war."

I thought about it as we drove past Child Drugs and the Marie Motel.

"Do you believe me?" she asked. "Do you know in your heart what I'm saying is true?"

"I do," I said. "I know you are true. I made the mistake of not trusting you once and it nearly got us killed. I won't make that mistake again."

Nearly got us killed? Nearly?

Sometimes, like in moments like these, I get the strangest, most dissonant feelings—almost like an existential echo—and I think that it wasn't *nearly*. That I had, in fact, gotten us killed, that wherever and whenever this was and however we were here, we were not, strictly speaking, among the living.

And as usual in these disconcerting turns of the dial that tuned in this eeriest of frequencies, I could've sworn I saw Ray Parker, my old partner and former Pinkerton, stepping out of the Marie and around the various people congregated there, giving me a quizzical look, then adjusting his hat and heading down Harrison in the night air thick with the threat of rain.

Like the night itself, the sensation was hypnotic and had a dreamlike quality.

Was I sleeping the sleep from which there was no waking, dreaming the dream of a world never to be born?

For in that sleep of death, what dreams may come?

"You okay?" Lauren said.

"Huh?"

"Where'd you go?"

"Sorry. What were you saying?"

"That Joan and girls like her—"

"Girls like her?" I asked.

"Girls there looking for something—a good time or a husband—don't get the boys to talk about home or the girls they left there. They talk intimately, romantically, as if they are the only two people on the planet, who need to embrace each other in this moment because they might not be here tomorrow."

I nodded.

"You sure you're okay?" she said.

"Yeah, sorry. Think Ray Parker just walked across my grave."

She shuddered at that.

"Thankfully it's us who get to walk across his—if we ever wanted to, which we will not. Let's change the subject. You think it's ever going to rain?"

"It's inevitable," I said, then thought, *Like death.* "It'll come in due time. Won't be much longer now."

"Needs to. The night needs the release."

I nodded my agreement, then said, "So Joan was looking?"

"I'm just saying she seemed to be. Could just be immature, needing of attention, restless, scared, bored, who knows? Usually if someone is really in a relationship—I mean all the way in—they don't seem to be single."

"True. What else?"

"I think she was acting strange in the week or so leading up to her disappearing, but only now in hindsight. I really didn't at the time."

I thought about it. "She may not even be missing. Just because Orca can't find her doesn't mean that she is."

"He seems like a nice guy, but . . . yeah, think I'd confirm she's actually missing before I did a whole lot. But if she is . . . I may just know who has her."

"Oh yeah? Who's that?"

"Don't know his name, but I'll try to find it out. Most of the boys cycle through, but the ones stationed here become regulars I guess. He must be stationed here. Used to come in and just stare at Joan for hours. I don't think he ever even spoke to her—not sure about that, but he was so creepy. Made her uncomfortable. Several of us spoke to him. Hell, a couple of the guys actually took him outside one night and gave him a stern talking to that included more than words. Next night he showed back up, black eye, bruised face and all, and just sat and stared all night."

"Ever see him with anyone else?"

"Never."

"Who would know who he is? When's the last time he was there? Was he in tonight?"

"Oh my God."

"What is it?"

"I just realized . . . He hasn't been back since she disappeared."

6

By the time we reached Gary and Rita's it was raining. Sheets of it sweeping in from St. Andrew's Bay.

They lived in a small house on 11th Street, which meant we were driving straight into the deluge, our vision as intermittent as the ineffective wipers impotently rubbing the windshield.

I parked on the opposite side of the street and we strained to see through the rain into the lives of others.

Gary's car wasn't parked in its usual spot beneath the carport, but through the large plate glass window in the front, we could see that Rita had made it back from her adventure at Nick's. She was pacing about the room, smoking, coming to the window often to look out into the rainy night, searching up and down 11th —for Gary or someone else?

"So she's home and he's not," Lauren said.

"Probably out looking for her."

"You've done all you can do for tonight," she said. "Take me home and make love to me."

Which, when Rita left the window again, I cranked up the car, drove us home, and did.

LAUREN and I lived in a small home on Grace Avenue not far from downtown. The place was modest in every way—particularly considering how much money Lauren had.

Of course, she had less now than she'd had just a short while ago, and at the rate she was giving it away, she'd soon have even less. It was a rare day that went by that she wasn't helping someone in need or funding an investigation she wanted me doing or contributing to the war effort in some way—all of which was fine by me. I didn't like the money or where it had come from, and had only made an uneasy peace with it so she could get the best medical treatment it could buy.

"This is my favorite time of day," she said.

Her naked body was draped across mine, her head on my chest, her hand tracing random designs on my skin.

"Mine too," I said. "Well, maybe a few minutes ago."

The room was dim but not dark, the streetlamps backlighting the rain on the windows casting shimmering patterns that danced across the walls and ceiling.

Charlie Christian and Benny Goodman were on the phonograph, way down low, barely audible above the rain.

"Sometimes I wonder why we ever do anything else," I said.

"It's the other things we do—doing our part—that helps make this so good."

"I don't think this needs any help being good," I said.

"You really think Rita is cheating on Gary?" she asked.

I shrugged, causing her head to rise a little. "My track record on such things is not so good."

"Thank God," she said.

"Do you really think she's not or do you just not want her to be?"

Now it was her turn to shrug. When she did, it caused her

breasts to caress my side—and I immediately tried to think of another question that would prompt the same response.

"I'm just not sure. How about Joan? You think she's gone off of her own accord, or was taken?"

"Of her own accord is most likely."

"Which means no happy ending for Ernie," she said.

"Not many of those."

"Not nearly enough."

I nodded.

"I used to think it was just the way of the world," she said. "That discontent and despair were sort of built in—goes along with the whole 'fallen world' notion. But now I really think it's just us. We just won't let ourselves be happy—always choosing things that take us away from instead of toward happiness."

"Not all of us," I said.

"No," she said, "not all of us."

And those were the last words we spoke on that or any other subject, as our breathing grew as heavy as our eyelids and we fell asleep entangled in each other to the sound of the night rain and Helen Forrest joining Benny Goodman on "Taking a Chance on Love."

I DREAMED OF CHILDHOOD.

A sunny day at the beach.

Me and Ernie and Orson swimming in the Gulf and playing in the sand—marco polo in the water, king of the mountain on the sand dunes, football on the beach.

Sandy. Sticky. Dried salt on our sunburned bodies. So much fun.

A kid we encountered had a pet seagull, and from the moment Orca saw it he wanted one. The kid, a boy a bit younger than us, whose name I couldn't recall, helped us catch one for Orca and clip his wings.

Even as a boy, Orson was enormous, and the small clipped-wing creature disappeared in the cradle formed by his huge hands.

As if born to care for the weak and defenseless, Orca stopped participating in all the activities, just so he could walk around holding his new pet, talking to the bird tenderly and gently caressing it with a single chubby finger.

When the sun was sinking and it was time to leave, Orca's grandmother, who was raising him and who had brought us to the beach, told him he wasn't allowed to carry the bird home.

But Grandma, I already clipped his wings, he explained.

Then you've killed the poor creature, she responded. Now put it down and let's go.

On the long, quiet drive back home, the only sound inside the car was Orson softy crying, an occasional sniffle, and his big hands wiping the tears streaming down his chubby cheeks.

On either side of the sad, large little boy, sat two average-sized lads, each with a consoling hand on his shoulder.

7

I t was nearly nine before I reached our offices the next morning.

I always intended to make it in earlier, but Lauren moved very slowly in the mornings, and the ministrations and medications always took longer than anticipated. I was glad she told Orson to come after nine.

Miki and Clip were already there waiting on me, Miki at her desk, Clip leaning against a nearby filing cabinet reading the paper.

If you looked closely enough, you could still see some puffiness in his face from his fight with Leonaldo Linderman, particularly around the patch over his missing eye.

I was worried about the damage the fight had done—and not just to his body.

Clipper Jones was a young black man who had been part of the 99th Fighter Squadron, 1st Tactical Unit before suffering the loss of his left eye. He picked up the nickname Clipper while training at Dale Mabry Field because of the way he would fly in low and clip the tops of the North Florida pine trees.

He was also my best friend and the best man I knew.

I had managed to beat Orson in, and I was glad for that.

As usual, Miki was wearing both a hat and sunglasses in an attempt to conceal the fact that she was Japanese.

The dark glasses hid her big, black, shy almond-shaped eyes, but not the cute oval face and flawless porcelain skin beneath the bangs of her shiny black hair.

Miki Matsumoto was a beautiful Japanese teen who, after having escaped the Japanese-American internment camp near Manzanar, had been in hiding on Panama City Beach with her family. From there she had been abducted, beaten, and repeatedly raped. I had found her and returned her to her family, but she later ran away from them when they had arranged a marriage for her with an old man because of what they referred to as *her shame*. She had shown up at my office and, after we had dealt with her family, was now working for me.

"Morning, boss," she said in her best Asian-Southern accent, which was getting better.

It was a big improvement over the *Morning Jimmy-san* she used to do while bowing.

She still bounced up out of her seat to greet me, but she didn't bow.

"Morning, Judy," I said, using the American name Lauren had given her.

"Jimmy," Clip said.

"Clip."

"Gentleman waiting in your office," he said.

Miki shot him a look. She wanted to be the one to tell me.

"Big guy?" I said. "Metal plate in his head? Answers to Orca?"

Clip shook his head. "Gary."

"Mr. Thomas," Miki said, shooting him another look.

He smiled.

"Thanks," I said.

"You expecting a whale-looking motherfucker?" he asked.

I nodded. "Tell him I won't be long."

"*I* will," Miki said.

~

GARY THOMAS LOOKED like he hadn't slept in a while. A long while.

Dark half-moons beneath bloodshot eyes, onion-paper skin, etched expressions, bone weariness.

"Where'd she go last night?" he asked the moment I walked in. "Who was she with? What did she do?"

"Where were you, Mr. Thomas?" I said, taking a seat behind my desk.

As usual, my desk was cluttered with a variety of books. I kept them close so even if I only had a random free moment here and there, I could read a snippet of something good, attempting to commit to memory that which was very good.

I slid the stack of books to one side so there were none between us.

As I did, he looked around my office, taking in all the other books that were piled, shelved, and stacked among the phonograph and records, chess set, filing cabinets, the framed photographs of Lauren, and the commendation I had received from the police department she had hung when I wasn't here.

"Who has time to read these days?" he said.

"I don't have as much as I would like," I said.

"What did you mean?" he asked. "Where was I?"

"It's a simple, straightforward question, Mr. Thomas. Where were you last night?"

"Out looking for her," he said. "How do you even know I wasn't home?"

"I went by your house to make sure she made it home safely," I said. "She was there. You weren't."

"Really?"

"Yes. Why?"

"What time was this?" he said.

"Why?"

"She wasn't home when I got there. I have no idea where she was and she never came back. I drove by her work this morning and she was there. Where did she go last night?"

"To the movies, then walking around downtown some."

"Who was she with?"

"She was alone," I said.

He shook his head. "Were you with her the whole time?"

"No."

"So she could've . . ."

"She didn't have enough time."

He shook his head again.

"Mr. Thomas—"

"Gary, for God's sakes—you're involved in the most intimate parts of my life."

"Gary . . . there's no evidence that your wife is cheating on you."

"She is. I know she is."

"Why don't you just talk to her?" I said. "If you both still want the relationship . . . I'm sure you can work it out. If either of you doesn't . . . it's best to let go and move on."

"Never. I'll never do that. She's my . . . I will never let her go."

"Mr. Thomas, when you say things like that, it makes me question whether I should continue working for you."

"You have to."

"No," I said. "I don't."

"I meant . . . I just meant . . . please help me. I need you to—"

"I'm trying, but you're not letting me."

"I'm . . . I'm just so . . . I can't think straight, can't . . ."

"I'll help you if you'll do what I tell you."

"Anything."

"Listen to me. You can't do anything until you know something, right? So stop worrying about it. Hell, stop even thinking about it. Just let it all go until you know something for sure. Can you do that? I want you to eat and sleep and occupy your mind with positive things, your body with positive activities, and just wait until I find out for sure what's going on. Will you do that?"

"I will," he said as if he actually intended to.

"No sign of the whale," Clip said.

Gary Thomas had just left and the three of us were standing out on the landing.

I looked at my watch. It was nearly ten.

"Would you mind making sure Mr. Thomas gets to work?" I said. "Then pick him back up tonight? See where he goes? What he's up to?"

"We following the clients now?" he said.

"It's a new service I'm thinking about offering. This is just a trial."

"Then I best not fuck it up."

After nodding to me and giving Miki a kiss goodbye, Clip eased down the stairs and out the front door to follow Gary Thomas.

The kiss had obviously embarrassed Miki, and she turned her flushed face away, looking toward her desk for something to do.

"How's he doing?" I asked.

"Still . . . sore," she said. "Blood in . . . urine and coughing."

"Keep a close eye on him. If he's still doing that in another day or so let's take him back to the doctor."

"Okie dokie, Jimmy boss-san."

"And Miki, I'm glad he kisses you goodbye. I hope he always does."

"Just . . . like you . . . and . . . Lady Boss Lauren."

"Speaking of . . ." I said.

I stepped back into my office and called Lauren.

"How're you feeling?" I said. "Did I wake you?"

"Been making some calls about Joan Wynn."

"Really? Thank you."

"Don't thank me yet. Haven't turned up anything so far. It's like she just vanished. I'll keep at it."

"Don't overdo it."

"I won't. I promise. What's your and Orson's first move?"

"*My* first move is to find Orson. He didn't show."

"Really? That's surprising."

"You have no idea," I said. "I've never known him to be late for anything."

"You worried?"

ORSON FERRELL HAD BEEN RAISED by his grandmother after his single mom left to buy eggs one day and never came back.

They lived in a small clapboard house on a dead-end side street in Springfield, not far from a laundromat.

Mary Francis Ferrell was a nervous, pale older woman with light freckles and a tight, high-pitched voice.

"Oh, Jimmy, I'm so glad you're lookin' for him. Yeah, I just don't know where that boy could be. No, he just never come home last night. Me, I didn't sleep a wink."

We were standing on her front screened-in porch surrounded by her mostly sandy yard. The rain was gone and the temperature had begun to drop. It still didn't feel like winter, but it was clearly headed in that direction.

"Has he been with you the entire time he's been back?"
I asked.

She shot me a surprised look. "Well, where else would he be?
Got nowhere else to go. You know that. He's too big to fit most
places, ain't he now? Lord, I'm so worried about that boy. My
mercy, I am."

"How long's he been back?"

"Week or so."

"And he hasn't done this before?"

Again, the same surprised look. "For heaven sakes, no. You
know how my Orson is. Always on time. Polite and considerate.
He wouldn't even stay out late for knowin' how it'd worry me."

In addition to the few sprigs of yellowing grass scattered
throughout the sand lot, a lone random palm tree stood near the
road, its fronds clacking occasionally in the breeze.

"What all's he done since he's been back?"

"Just look for that girl. Night and day. Worrying himself sick
over Ernie's girl. Doesn't that just beat all? But ain't that just like
our Orson? No time to get a girl of his own—not that any girl
would have the big buffoon—'cause he's trying to take care of his
best friend's girl."

I nodded and thought about it.

"I'm worried Jimmy," she said. "Real worried."

"I'll—"

She lowered her voice even though no one was around and
the lots on either side of hers were vacant. "He's different now.
Come back different from over there. Won't talk about what
happened or what he seen, but it changed him. That's a fact."

"How so?"

"Nightmares every night. Short fuse. Set off by the strangest
little things. Sort of not there much of the time. Catch him just
staring off. At nothing. He'd do it for hours if I didn't stop him,
bring him back down to earth. Keep waiting for my sweet boy to
show up, but so far ... he's ... just ... gone."

"Gary's at work," Clip said when I got back to the office. "He walked by his wife's place and made sure she there first, then strolled his suspicious ass on to his damn job."

"Thanks."

"Henry Mr. Folsom call you," Miki said.

"The *Mr.* go in front," Clip told her.

"Mr. Henry Folsom call you," she said.

"That's good," Clip said, "but no need to call that bastard *Mr.* at all."

She looked confused.

"Just say Henry Bastard Folsom," he said.

"You do realize she's our receptionist, don't you?" I asked.

He smiled.

"What did *Detective* Folsom say?" I asked Miki.

"Say he need ah see you. Possible soonest."

I nodded. "Thank you."

I walked into my office to call Folsom back and Clip followed me.

"She say you went out looking for the whale," he said.

"Never showed up this morning," I said. "His grandmother said he never came home last night."

"So the person looking for the missing person is missing?"

"Uh huh."

"Well hell. How about that?"

I nodded.

"Want me to go find him?" he asked.

"Figured that might be something we do together after I call Folsom."

"That bastard," he said.

I smiled. "A guy tries to kill you once and you hold it against him the rest of your life, don't you?"

He laughed as he turned to leave.

"Hey," I said, "before you go. Something I've been wanting to talk to you about."

"Okay," he said, holding his hands up in a placating gesture, "I'll quit fuckin' with Miki's English."

"That's not English," I said. "And not what I wanted to talk to you about."

"What's up?"

"We just sort of fell into this thing," I said, indicating the offices. "Never really talked about it."

"Fine by me we leave it that way."

"Can't do that."

"Didn't figure you could," he said.

"Goes without saying—"

"Evidently not."

I laughed.

"Read too much," he said. "Talk too much. Think too much."

"So I've been told. Thing is . . . I want you workin' *with* me not *for* me."

"I kinda thought you's workin' for me," he said.

The smile that flashed on his face made him look like a kid.

"I want you to have the other office," I said.

"Ray's office?"

"You've always been far more a partner to me than he ever was," I said.

He nodded and something flickered in his eyes that said more than any words ever could.

"But damn, Jimmy," he said, "the hell I gonna do with a office?"

"Call Miki in for dictation," I said, careful to keep my voice and face serious.

He smiled an even bigger smile than before. "Guess maybe I *do* need a office."

He walked out, shaking his head to himself. "Dictation," he said under his breath. "*Shee-it.*"

As he reached the door, Henry Folsom was standing there.

"Clip," he said.

Clip didn't say anything.

Miki stepped around Folsom and said, "Folsom Mr. Bastard here see you."

Ignoring them both, Folsom stepped into my office.

"Jimmy," he said.

Henry Folsom and I had history.

He had been my boss for a while when I was a cop. He had been more like a father to me than a boss. He had been a good man and a righteous cop until, compromised by his wife's poor health, he had turned a blind eye to war profiteering and a robust black market, and had actually conspired to get me, Clip, and Lauren killed.

Lauren understood and had forgiven him. I didn't understand and would never trust him again, but was trying to let it go. Clip never would.

He was a tall, thick middle-aged man with big, thick hands— one of which was holding something that looked like a chunk of coal.

"You're a little late for Christmas," I said.

He looked down at the coal in his hand and smiled.

"Or is that what you got?"

He let out a deep sigh and shook his head.

"Yeah, Jimmy, it's what I got," he said in his most world-weary voice. "I'm a bad guy for trying to take care of my wife."

"What can I do for you, Henry?"

"I came to ask for your help—not for me, but for your country —but I can see it was a mistake."

"You give up awful easy," I said.

"I'm old and tired. Don't have the stamina I used to."

He looked old and tired. Shoulders hunched in and back bent ever so slightly, perpetually furrowed forehead, deep lines on his face that looked more like scars than wrinkles.

"Turn that around," I said, nodding to the coal. "Is that what I think it is?"

"I wondered if you'd remember," he said.

He placed the brick of coal on the front edge of my desk, turning it so I could see the other side.

Explosives had been pressed into a hollowed-out section of

the fake coal—something that could only be seen from the side that now faced me.

Back in June of '42, four German men floated to shore at Ponte Vedra Beach on a rubber raft from a U-boat off the coast. They quickly unloaded and buried four boxes containing explosives and nearly two hundred thousand dollars in US currency.

In civilian clothes and with American money, the four men made their way to an isolated grocery store and purchased bus tickets to Jacksonville. In Jacksonville, they bought train tickets to New York and Chicago and set off in pairs to those destinations.

The four men, who spoke nearly perfect English and had actually lived in the US before, were recruited to sabotage American industries, not only to slow the war effort but to strike terror in the hearts of American citizens.

The explosives disguised as pieces of coal were to be put in trains to explode when they reached the right temperature.

The plot, which was designed by the Abwehr, the German military intelligence agency, never went off because one of the saboteurs, the main mission leader, in fact, a man named Georg Johann Dacsh, turned himself in to the FBI and revealed the plan after only thirty hours in the US.

I was a still a cop at the time, and Folsom and I had been alerted to be on the lookout for similar operations coming ashore on our beaches.

"They're at it again," Folsom said. "Beach patrol in St. Petersburg intercepted men attempting to carry out a very similar plan. Under interrogation, one of the men said that other teams were coming ashore on other beaches around Florida, including ours. Said this time their plan is to blow up shipyards, and air force and naval bases, and train lines in and around the beaches where they land. Said their mistake last time had been asking the men to travel so far—gave 'em too much time to think about what they were doing. This time they plan to carry out the plot close to where they come ashore."

I nodded. "It's a better plan."

"If there was a massive attack on Wainwright Shipyard or Tyndall Field or the Naval Section Base," he said, "it'd be devastating to both our community and the war effort. If they successfully carried out several across the state or even the country, we could lose the war."

He was right.

"I'm shorthanded," he said. "Plus my men look like cops. You and Clip, Lauren and Judy—or whatever her name is—don't. Y'all might be able to find out things we can't. Figured you might ask for additional help from some of your and Clip's, ah, acquaintances."

I thought about it. He meant the marginalized of our town, the lower class and even criminal element.

"I'm not asking for me," he said. "I'm asking for our country."

"And," I said, "that's exactly who we'll do it for."

11

"Don't tell me you trust him," Clip said.

"Hell no."

"Bet it some kinda setup."

"Could be," I said. "But I can't find the angle in it if it is. I worked the previous plot. It was legit."

"Last one bein' legit don't mean this one is," he said.

"True."

We were in my car, driving down Grace Avenue on our way to pick up Lauren. Once we were out of downtown, there was no traffic at all. The day was clear and cool, sunny, but the temperature was dropping.

"And I ain't puttin' Miki in danger even if it is," he said.

I nodded. It went without saying that I felt the same way about Lauren. And though Clip wouldn't know it, not only did some things go without saying, but I actually left some of them unsaid.

The plan was to pick up Lauren and have her accompany us to the USO to get more information about Joan and to see if anyone saw which way Orson headed after we left last night.

"We gots enough to do as it is," he added. "Missing girls and whales, tailing the unhappy wives of unhappier husbands."

"I know," I said. "We've got more than enough to do. It could be a setup. But I think we need to do it anyway. If it's a real threat . . . think about the lives that would be lost, the damage that could be done, the impact on the war."

He seemed to be thinking about it.

"Look," I said. "You don't have to do anything. Just keep it in mind. You hear something, see something . . . let me know."

"I can do that," he said. "Now back to our real work. We lookin' for the girl or the whale?"

"We look for the guy, we might find him," I said. "We look for the girl, we might find them both."

He nodded.

Lauren was ready and waiting when we arrived.

As if a choreographed routine we'd done a thousand times, Clip and I quickly got out, and as I rounded the front of the car, he slipped into the backseat. I then kissed Lauren and helped her into the car, closing my door just a few seconds after closing hers.

"Miki just called," Lauren said. "Orson's grandmother called the office and said he was home. Asked if you'd come talk to him."

"She say anything else?"

"Says he can't remember much of anything from last night and doesn't remember driving home."

I nodded.

"Why don't you drop me at the club and I'll ask around about Joan while you two go talk to him?"

Which was exactly what we did.

"SOMETHING'S wrong with my head, Jimmy," Orson said.

He had met us when we pulled up and we were now leaning on the car talking.

My guess was he didn't want his grandmother hearing what he had to say.

The late afternoon light made everything glow softly, imbuing everything with a gentle golden beauty. The cool air was thin and crisp, pleasant and easy to breathe, and the slight breeze stirred things about, tousled my hair—Orca's and Clip's were too short for such an effect—and caused the palm fronds to flap intermittently.

"It's all messed up."

"Whatta you mean?"

"I keep losing time," he said. "Keep comin' to and can't remember where I been or what I been doin'."

He had just met Clip for the first time, but if he minded talking in front of him he gave no indication.

"What do you remember about last night?"

"Runnin' into you at that little bar. What's the name of it?"

"Nick's."

"Yeah, Nick's. Bopping that asshole on his head. Drinkin' with that girl."

"What girl?" I asked.

He squinted then shook his head. "Was that last night?"

"We walked outside and talked," I said. "Remember?"

"Oh yeah," he said. "That's right. We talked."

"Then what'd we do?"

His huge, round face narrowed in focus.

"We went somewhere," he said. "Where'd we go? Oh yeah, I met your girl. Laura."

"Lauren."

"Lauren, right."

"Do you remember where that was?" I asked.

"Under the flagpole."

"That's right. Where?"

"Near the water," he said. "The USO club."

"Exactly," I said. "Then Lauren and I left. What'd you do then?"

He shook his head. "I can't . . . I just don't know. What did I do? Why can't I remember? What's wrong with me?"

He hit himself on the head with his closed fist.

"Just relax," I said. "No pressure. No big deal. We'll figure it out. How often does this happen? When did it start?"

"Just since I been back— The USO Club. I went inside. After you and Laura left I went inside. I asked around about Ernie's girl, Joan."

"That's good. See? You're doing good."

"Nobody knew nothin'," he said. "Or if they did they weren't spillin'."

"Then what'd you do?"

He thought about it for a while, then shook his head. "I don't know. I can't remember. Wait. I wanted a drink—a real drink."

"Where'd you go for that?"

He thought about it some more, the furrow of concentration just above and between his eyes a puffy, pronounced ridge with two deep lines on either side.

Eventually, he shook his head. "I just . . . don't know. Where . . . wait. The same place we had been. What was the name of it?"

"Nick's?"

"Yeah, Nick's. I had a drink with that girl."

"What girl?"

He shook his head. "That's . . . all I . . . got. Need to . . . lie . . . down."

I pressed him a little more, but got nothing else.

"Get some sleep big fella," I said. "Call me when you get up and we'll see if we can't figure out what else happened last night. And we'll find Joan."

"Joan," he said, as if he had forgotten. "Oh no. I can't rest. I've got to find Joan."

"We're going to look for her right now," I said. "You go get some rest. I'll call if you we turn up anything. If you don't hear from me, call me when you get up and you can join the search."

"You're a real pal, Jimmy. A real pal. Always have been."

Without saying anything else, he turned unsteadily and stumbled across the small sandy yard, up the stairs, through the porch, and back into the house.

We watched him as he did, and for a long moment after he was inside, we just stood there staring after him.

"The hell happen to him over there?" Clip said.

"We need to find out," I said.

"He wasn't like that before?"

I shook my head. "Not at all. That was like talking to someone who *looks* like my old friend, not my friend himself, not Orca. A stranger bearing a striking resemblance."

12

J oan Wynn lived with her aunt off Cherry Street in the Cove, not far from where I used to live in the Cove Hotel.

The small block home was modest, but nice, and sported a fresh coat of paint—white on the blocks and yellow on the shutters.

Inside, what little furniture there was had never been nice, and it had been decades since it had seen better days.

"I've worried myself sick over that girl," Lilium Wynn said. "I've got such a bad feeling."

Lilium Wynn, Joan's dad's sister who had never married or had kids of her own, looked like the flower she was named after—pale and frail, dainty and delicate. She must have been a good deal older than Joan's dad, who had been killed along with her mother in a house fire, because she was quite elderly—perhaps as old as her midseventies. She was tall and thin, with light freckles largely hidden by makeup and sky-blue eyes largely hidden by glasses.

Looking at her and thinking about the flower she was named after, I realized the exterior color scheme of her house also mimicked her namesake flower.

"When's the last time you saw her?" I asked.

She glanced over at Clip again—something she had been doing without much subtlety since we'd arrived.

"A week ago yesterday. She left in the evening to do her volunteer work at the USO and the next morning when I woke up she wasn't here. I guess she could've come back during that time and left again. I just don't know. But if she did, she left earlier than she normally did—and without a word to me."

"Does she have a car?"

She nodded. "Her parents left her a little money and their old car."

"Do you know the make and model?"

"I'm sorry, I don't. It's black. A Ford maybe. I'm just not certain."

"Has she ever gone off before?" I asked.

"She's a good girl," she said. "Just . . . a little impulsive. She's gone to a girlfriend's place before and forgotten to call until the next morning, but never more than that. Never anything like this."

"Do you have any idea where she might be?"

"I've called everyone I can think of," she said. "No one's seen her. Like I said, I've told all this to the police."

"I know, and I appreciate you telling us again. It helps. It really does."

"Sure," she said, nodding her head slightly, as if it were barely attached. "Anything for a friend of Ernie's. Ernie's got such good friends. That big one is very nice too. He's also trying to find my Joan for me. Ernie and Joan make such a good couple. None of this would've happened if he was here. He helped keep her . . . occupied. A girl like her needs that. The firm hand of a good man."

I had never thought of Ernie's hand as being particularly firm, but then I had never been his girlfriend either.

"We've got to find her before he gets back," she said. "No matter where she is."

There was something in that.

"Whatta you mean?"

"Pardon?" she said.

"Whatta you mean 'no matter where she is'?"

"Just that. They'll be so happy once they're together. We've just got to get them back together. He's gonna need her to care for him when he gets back, now that he's injured."

She glanced from my missing right arm to Clip's eyepatch.

"Miss Wynn, all I care about is finding her and making sure she's safe," I said. "It doesn't matter where she is. My associate and I are very discreet. We wouldn't embarrass Joan or do anything to expose anything you or she might not want made public."

"I'm sure I don't know what you mean," she said.

"Okay. May we look in her room?"

She looked at Clip again. "I'd rather you not."

"It would really help," I said. "Could be the thing that helps us find her."

"It just wouldn't be appropriate," she said. "Two . . . men . . . going through her private things."

"My wife helps me sometimes," I said. "Would it be all right if I brought her back and let her have a look around?"

She thought about it.

Lauren and I weren't married, but that didn't make her any less my wife—and though *wife* wasn't a strong or significant enough word, it was a shorthand most people could understand.

"I guess that might be all right," she said. "If you really think it'll help find her."

13

"He seemed real agitated," Lottie Brusher said. "I tried to talk to him, see what was the matter, calm him down some, you know? But . . . nothin' seemed to help."

Lottie Brusher, the young, wide-eyed, energetic wartime volunteer was talking about Orson, and how he had acted when he came to the USO club after Lauren and I left last night.

We had found her in a lookout tower on the beach and climbed up to talk to her.

"Any idea what had him agitated?" I asked. "He seemed fine when we left."

"He seemed fine when he first came in," she said, "then out of the blue, all of a sudden, for no reason, he just grew real screwy."

The large wooden tower we were in resembled a lifeguard tower—only bigger. Four long telephone poles extended up some thirty feet from a cement pilings foundation to a square wooden platform atop which was a small wooden enclosure with a tin roof.

The lookout towers had been constructed for spotters to watch the waters surrounding our peninsula for submarines, in particular the U-boats that kept taking out our tankers.

The beaches of Florida were littered with them.

"Missy, you volunteer here durin' the day and down to the USO at night?" Clip asked.

She nodded as if it were no big deal.

"People like you are the reason we're gonna win the war," I said.

"Wow, thanks soldier, but you brave boys are the real reason we're gonna win."

I lifted my right shoulder and what remained of my arm. "This happened here," I said. "Never got the chance to go over and serve."

"Oh. Sorry."

"Thanks."

"Lost my eye servin'," Clip said.

"Good for you," she said. "I mean . . . I just meant . . ."

"We know what you meant," I said. "It's fine. So Orson got agitated for no reason, then what?"

"Well, like I said I tried to calm him down, but he was havin' none of it. He didn't stay long. Right in the middle of conversation —well, of me talking—he stood up and said he was going back to Nick's for a real drink, did I want to go. I told him I couldn't and that he shouldn't either. He said something about Nick's having real women too, then stormed out."

The temperature was continuing to drop with the late afternoon sun, which with the gusts of wind made the drafty enclosure we were standing in feel like a large ice box.

The natural pause in our conversation provided the perfect place for Lottie to do what she was up here to do. Lifting the large binoculars, she stepped through the open doorway of the box and over to the railing surrounding the platform.

We followed her out onto the platform and followed her gaze across the Gulf.

Beyond the calm blue-green waters and the gently undulating

waves patting the shore, the sun was sinking into the vanishing point of the horizon off to the west.

We could see for miles and miles and I wondered how many German subs were beneath the surface of the waters visible to us at the moment.

Glancing away from the Gulf, I looked down the beach to the east, back toward town. In the far distance I could see another tower like the one we were in. Between here and there, the naval horseback patrol strolled along the empty coastline, the sand so white the horses' hooves appeared to be trotting in sugar.

After finishing her scan of the Gulf, Lottie walked back inside. We followed.

She replaced the big binoculars on the small stand, shivered a bit, rubbed her hands together, and pulled her jacket up around her.

"Lauren said you knew Joan Wynn pretty well and could tell us about her too," I said.

Lottie shrugged. "Knew her a little. Not sure I can tell you much."

"Do you mind just starting by telling us your opinion of her, your impression?"

"Well ... let's see. Joan ... She's not a bad egg, just sort of restless, you know? Like bored with life most of the time. Lookin' for ... I don't know ... somethin', anything to occupy her. You know what I mean?"

"I know exactly what you mean," I said.

"I don't," Clip said. "Must be a white people thing."

Lottie wasn't sure how to take that. She glanced quickly from Clip to me, patted down her pin curls, pulled her jacket up around her again, and proceeded.

"Like I said, she wasn't bad, but ... boredom can get you into trouble if you're not careful. What's that saying? Idle hands are the devil's workshop."

"That's it," I said, nodding.

"Jimmy here got less for the devil to work with these days," Clip said.

I smiled. "Smaller workshop but more efficient," I said.

Lottie, uncertain how to take Clip's comment—or Clip for that matter—smiled awkwardly.

"I like Joan. I do. But she can be tiring. Always wanting something else, always looking for . . . a new something, a new anything. Lately, she wanted to be in pictures. I said you have to move to Hollywood for that and she said she just might do that. She's pretty enough, kinda glamourous, but I don't know if she can act or . . . I mean, you have to be . . . I mean to be in pictures."

"What did you think when she stopped volunteering at the USO?"

She shrugged. "That she found something new to occupy her for a bit. I just hoped it wasn't one of those fly boys who fawned over her."

"Know any of their names?"

She shook her head. "I hoped maybe she started volunteering somewhere else or maybe her fella came home early. I thought maybe, just maybe, she really did go to Hollywood. She's . . . I wouldn't be shocked if she did. I wouldn't."

"What about the guy who came in and stared at her? Know anything about him?"

"Oh wow, I had forgotten about him. If it's who I think you mean. Lots of guys stared at her. Lots of guys stare at Lauren. You're a very lucky man. But, yeah, there was the one guy who only stared. Never did anything else."

"Know his name or anything about him?"

"You don't think he could've . . ."

"Wants to have a little chat with him either way," Clip said.

"Oh I wish y'all would, but I don't know anything about him."

"Who would?"

"A couple of the fellas finally tossed him out. They talked to him more than anyone. What were their names? Oh Gosh, that was right before Joan stopped coming. Oh my."

"Their names?"

"Who?"

"The guys who threw him out?"

"They were navy guys. Mom would know."

I knew she meant Mildred Wade, the most senior hostess of the USO and not her own mother. All the girls—the junior and senior hostesses—called her Mom.

"Tell Lauren to introduce you. Talk to her. She'll know. Oh Gosh, I hope he didn't . . . I hope she's not with him."

14

Later that afternoon, Clip and I picked up Lauren and went shopping.

One of the many amazing things Lauren did with her money was buying supplies for the USO Clubs in town—both the white club on Harrison and the Negro club on 6th Street. On occasion she even used her own rationing tickets to get certain items she wanted the boys to have. And she always got the exact same things for both clubs.

"There shouldn't be separate clubs," she had said, "but as long as there are, they're going to have the same supplies."

The three of us unloaded the bags and boxes filled with everything from staples to soda at the USO on 6th, then headed to the one on Harrison, hoping to talk to Mildred after we unloaded there.

"You do all this 'cause you feel guilty 'about somethin'?" Clip said.

Lauren smiled. "Not guilty, grateful."

He nodded.

"I know it take a toll on you," he said. "See how tired you get."

"Do not grow weary in well doing," she said. "I just keep

reminding myself of that—that *and* service is the rent we pay for citizenship."

"You gots the highest rent of anyone I know."

"But I can afford it," she said with a smile.

"We all be able to you keep passin' out those big stacks of bills," he said. "Hell, you got me and Miki thinkin' 'bout buying a house."

"Oh, Clip, you should," she said. "You really should."

"Ain't sure 'bout gettin' that damn domesticated," he said.

"You could sleep outside and use an outhouse if that'd make you feel better," I said.

"That what you do?"

Before I could respond, we were pulling up in front of the USO on Harrison and I could see that David Howell was waiting for us.

David Howell was a quiet, youngish cop who worked for Henry Folsom. He was tall and too thin and walked with a slight limp as the result of his service overseas, which he never spoke about.

"Got a minute?" he said as I got out of the car.

As usual, he was simply but impeccably dressed in a dark suit, white shirt, and dark tie. Every hair was in place, and he stood as erect as anyone I knew.

I nodded. "Just let me help get the supplies in first."

"I'll help too," he said, and did.

When we were done, he said, "Take a little walk with me?"

I turned to Lauren. "You okay here for a little while?"

"I was just gonna stay and start my shift early anyway," she said.

"I'll check on you later when I come back to talk to Mildred."

"Sounds swell," she said. "Be careful and miss me."

"Always do the former because of the latter," I said.

We then kissed and I turned to leave.

As Howell and I started walking way, Clip just stood there, seemingly not sure what to do.

I turned back toward Clip.

"You want me to head back to the office?" he asked.

I looked at Howell. "This *is* official, right?"

He nodded.

"Then Clip is with us. He's a full partner in our agency."

Howell nodded and Clip joined us. We walked slowly, letting Howell set the pace with his slightly halting and awkward gait.

"Where we headed?" I asked.

"Crime scene not far from here," he said.

He led us back up Harrison toward Beach.

"Mind if we talk about Joan Wynn on the way?"

"Not at all," he said. "I heard you were helping the big fella look for her. How's that going?"

"Just started but got nothing so far. You?"

"The girl just vanished," he said. "Haven't found a single trace of her. Got no leads. Not a single one. Nothing."

When we reached Beach Drive we took a left, then a right behind some buildings and over to Oak.

"Which means she either wanted to disappear," I said, "someone took her and made her disappear, or she's dead somewhere and just hasn't been found yet."

He nodded. "That's the way I got it figured."

"Got a frontrunner for one of those?"

"Got nothin'," he said. "I told you. And it's not from lack of looking."

We took Oak to 4th and when we turned on 4th, my heart sank a little.

"Where we headed?" I asked.

"Vacant lot over here on the other side of that warehouse."

It was the place where Betsy had disappeared into the darkness with the john when I was out here on the sidewalk talking to Orson last night.

"Is it Betsy?" I asked.

He stopped walking. "What can you tell me about it? How'd you know?"

"Saw her go in here with a john last night. Figured she used this spot a lot. Odds were good it was her. High-risk work."

"Witnesses say they saw you two together at Nick's," he said.

"We were both sitting at the bar," I said. "We were next to each other. I even bought her a drink. We weren't together. I was working. And I guess so was she."

He nodded. "I don't suspect you. I just wondered if you could tell me anything you remember from last night?"

"How was she killed?"

"See for yourself," he said, ushering us onto the vacant lot. "But brace yourselves—she was beaten to death, and the guy took his time and did it right."

We walked past a few cops in the front of the lot to a few more cops with the coroner in the back.

Betsy was so badly beaten I had to take Howell's word for it that it was her. Her bruised and bloodied head was misshapen, kind of oblong and egg-shaped, her eyes swollen shut in large puffy purple masses. Her clothes were still on, but torn and ripped, lifted and shoved aside to reveal her breasts and genitals.

"Got damn," Clip said, whistling softly.

"It's bad," I said.

"Bad? That the worse shit I ever seen," Clip said. "And I seen some bad shit."

"Worse than anything I ever saw in the war," Howell said. "Even guys sitting there with their arms blown off. As if just remembering my arm, he glanced at it, then away, and flushed. "I just meant . . ."

"Don't feel like you have to dance around it. It's gone. No big deal."

"It a big deal when you tryin' to hang wallpaper," Clip said.

"True."

"Just like my missin' eye a big deal when I tries to wink. Or see a right hook coming."

"I could've said *legs*," Howell said. "Like mine. I should have. I don't know why I didn't."

"Seriously," I said, "I'd really appreciate it if you wouldn't try to dance around it. I'd rather you joke about it like Clip does."

"I wasn't jokin'," Clip said. "I gets tired of havin' to hang all the wallpaper."

We laughed.

"Have any idea when she was killed?" I asked.

"She was seen back at the bar after you left," he said. "She drank some more, tried to find some more work, but it wasn't until your friend, the big fella, came back that she struck it lucky. Or was it unlucky? They drank together for a while. Then she left with him around midnight and was never seen alive again."

15

Dusk growing toward dark.

A cold, brisk breeze blew trash and leaves and bits of sand around the lot and out onto 4th Street.

Visibility was decreasing quickly.

I scanned the lot again.

It was mostly sandy soil, but there were also some clumps of grass and weeds scattered about, yellow-brown, brittle, waving wanly in the wind.

The entire lot was clearly visible from 4th Street, and would be somewhere Betsy could only use at night.

At night, there would be plenty of cover of darkness toward the back or on the side next to the warehouse for the services she was paid to render.

Howell had invited us to look around, and we were. When the light was gone so was the scene and any evidence it might contain.

I looked at the body again.

"Do you know what time it stopped raining?" I asked Clip.

"Didn't think it did 'til mornin'," he said. "She dry, ain't she?"

"Mostly, yeah."

"That what, in the peeper trade, we calls a clue."

"You're a natural," I said.

While the cops were focused on the body and the lot, we walked over to get a better look at the warehouse.

It was a large two-story tin building with a sliding cargo door on the side next to the empty lot.

"Look at that," I said to Clip.

There in the dirt near the door were a man's footprints and two long narrow and shallow trenches like the heel marks of someone being dragged.

"You mind trying the door?" I said.

He did.

It slid open easily.

"Got something?" Howell yelled from across the way.

"Careful not to step on the tracks in front of the door," I said, then we stepped inside.

The warehouse was obviously just for storage of old stuff and not used on a regular basis—except by Betsy. To the right of the door on the floor was a pallet of blankets and a pillow. Next to it, an overturned crate serving as a nightstand held a candle, a bottle of cheap booze, and a book of matches.

"No wonder the body's dry," Howell said, coming up behind us. "She had a regular little hot-sheet hotel rent free right here." He turned to one of the other cops who had just entered the building. "Find out who owns this place and what they know about this."

"Anybody she ever brought here knew about it," I said. "Could easily hide and watch, attack her when the john left."

"Sure," Howell said, "but it makes more sense that it was one she was with."

I shrugged.

"I know you don't want it to be your friend, but . . ."

"Just looking at everything, considering all possibilities that occur to me," I said. "Know better than not to."

"You're right about that."

"Lots of suspects when a working girl's killed," I said. "Could be any of a number of sad, lonely, frustrated, drunk, angry guys."

"Yeah, or it could be the one she was last seen with."

"Could be," I said. "Any evidence that it is?"

"I don't see a note or nothing," he said.

"Did you notice the footprints?" I asked.

He turned back to look and we stepped over to the open door.

"They're big," I said, "but nowhere as big as Orson's."

"Huh," he said, lifting his hat and rubbing his head. To the other officers he said, "Get pictures of all these—and the setup inside."

The cop with the camera walked over and began doing just that.

"I want measurements too. Casts if we can swing it. And make sure they're not bigger than they look and just got pushed down some. That's what it looks like to me."

He turned back to me. "Seen enough?"

I nodded.

"I'll walk y'all out."

He made a move out of the warehouse and toward the front of the lot, and we followed.

"Did you find her purse?" I asked. "Any money on her?"

He shook his head. "Not so far."

"So it could be a robbery."

"Could be," he said. "It could be. Or it could be meant to look like it."

"WE HAVEN'T KNOWN each other long," Howell said.

He, Clip, and I were standing on the sidewalk on 4th Street down a little ways from the lot and away from the other cops.

"But I think we're both honest and try to do the right thing."

I nodded.

"I'm gonna conduct a thorough investigation," he said. "Follow where it leads me—no matter where that is. And right now it looks to be leading toward your friend. Just wanted you to know."

"You've got an eyewitness that puts them together," I said. "Same as me."

"Not the same," he said. "Much later and he's the last person she was seen with. Seen *leaving* with."

"But that's it," I said. "That's all you got. There's plenty that points in other directions—and it's far better evidence than someone seeing them leaving a bar together. The footprints, the body being dry, the missing purse."

"I'm not saying it's him," he said. "I'm saying he's a suspect— my *prime* suspect—and I just wanted you to know."

"The guy I knew before the war could never do something like that," I said. "I don't know about the guy who came back. But I doubt he could either. I doubt the war could change a man that much."

"That's because you weren't over there in it," he said.

16

Clip and I walked back to the USO, but instead of going in, we got in my car and drove back over to Orson's.

"You a'right?" Clip asked.

We were on 6th Street in light traffic.

I nodded.

"What did you see over there?" I asked. "Could the war change the sweetest guy I knew growing up into a monster who could do that?"

"Clouds," he said. "All I saw was clouds. I's high up in the sky in a metal bird. But stories I heard . . . directly from the guys what lived them . . . yeah, it could."

"It'll take a lot more evidence to convince me."

"Question is, could any amount?"

I nodded again. "Sure. If the evidence says so or if he tells me . . . then, yeah. I'll believe it."

"Well, let's see what he has to say."

～

"Jimmy, I swear to God I can't remember," Orson was saying.

We were outside again, out of reach of his grandmother's earshot.

"Have you remembered anything else?" I asked.

"I remember things, but I don't know which night they go with."

"Like what?"

"I don't know, just . . . Like I remember this guy borrowing a buck from me, but I don't know when it was."

"At Nick's? Do you know him?"

"I was drinking . . . but I don't think it was Nick's. I didn't know him. He just looked thirsty. Wait. Maybe . . . it could've been at the USO. I'm just not positive."

"But he wouldn't need money at the USO," I said.

"Oh yeah. I just . . . I don't know. I can't remember. It's like everything is loose inside my head and somebody jumbled it up and now it's all mixed up."

"Did you go back to Nick's and talk to Betsy?" I said. "Did you leave with her? Did you and she . . . have sex?"

"I wanted to," he said. "I just don't know if I did."

"It was raining," I said. "You got wet. Where did you go? Who were you with?"

"Jimmy, I just can't remember," he said, hitting his head with his fist. "I can't. I'm sorry. I wish to God I could. One way or another. I don't want to have done it, but I want to know. Either way, I want to know."

"Either way," I said, "we're gonna find out."

"Can we keep looking for Joan while we do?"

"*We?*"

"Yeah. I'll help you find out who killed Betsy—even if it was me—and you help me find out where Joan is."

"I don't know, Orca," I said. "I don't think it's you, but what if it is?"

"Then who better to help you prove it?" he said. "And if it was me, I will. I'll help you prove it and turn myself in. You know I will. If I did it, I didn't mean to, didn't know I was, and wouldn't be able to live with myself, so I'd want to turn myself in anyway. Come on, Jimmy, you know that's the truth. Besides, if I'm with you, you can keep an eye on me."

I knew what he was saying was true.

"Okay," I said.

Which was how half an hour later, after dropping Clip off at the office, Orson and I were back at the USO talking to Mildred Wade while Clip and Miki were tailing Gary and Rita Thomas.

17

"Lauren's told you what we're up against, right?" Mildred Wade asked.

Orson and I were standing out front of the USO with Mildred Wade, a tall, very thin older woman with a long neck, a small head, and a raspy voice as if she had smoked or yelled too much. Her short, gray-brown hair was plastered to her head like a flying helmet—an illusion aided by her large black glasses that resembled pilot goggles.

I nodded.

An enemy nearly as dangerous as the Germans or the Japs— but far more covert—were all the victory girls and good-time Charlottes, the hardened professionals like Betsy, the idealistic amateurs, the lonely widows and wives, and the sexual diseases being transmitted to our troops. An army doctor who treated VD had put it just right: "While mothers are winning the war in the factories, their daughters are losing it on the streets." Because Florida was the site of so much military training, our state was an epicenter for venereal disease. In addition to everything else they did, the USO clubs were meant to keep our boys out of bars and brothels in order to keep disease and infection out of them.

"We don't call it VJ Day, we call it VD Day," Mildrid said.

She showed no signs of embarrassment, and didn't even lower her voice so that the parade of young servicemen passing by us on their way into or out of the club wouldn't hear.

"It's an epidemic. It could cost us the war—and that's no exaggeration. So we offer an alternative. A safe, wholesome place for the boys to unwind and have fun. They also get the feeling of home and get reminded of what they're fighting for. Women like Lauren and me remind them of their mothers."

Mildred was much older than Lauren, but even in her prime couldn't compare. I was fairly certain Lauren didn't remind any of the boys of their mothers.

"Sure, she's young and beautiful, but she carries herself in such a way . . . She's very maternal."

"Thank you," I said. "I'm very proud of the work she's doing."

"You should be. It's not easy—and with her health . . ."

I nodded.

The night was cold, and Mildred didn't have a jacket, but didn't seem to need one. She had refused the offer of ours and appeared unfazed.

"The young girls, the junior hostesses, have a slightly different role . . . They should remind the boys of their kid sisters or the girl next door or even their sweetheart—but only in the most wholesome of ways. That's why this work's not for every young woman."

She paused and in the intervening silence I could hear music and dancing from inside the club, the splash of the bay waters beyond, a foghorn in the distance, and the nocturnal sounds of the city behind us—traffic, horns, people bustling about, laughter, and the occasional yell or whistle.

The sounds were various, but the smell singular. The cold night air carried on its currents the briny scent of the bay. Salty with a touch of tang.

She didn't say anything else so I said, "Tell us about Joan Wynn."

"She wasn't particularly suited for it," she said.

"You ain't sayin' she did anything to dishonor Ernie, are you?" Orson said.

He leaned forward slightly when he said it, his body growing tense, his voice conveying something like challenge if not actual menace.

"Let her say what she means, big guy," I said. "We want the truth. No matter what it is. Remember? Don't make her hesitant to tell it."

"I ain't hesitant," Mildred said. "He don't scare me none. I deal with big boys like him every single day. Can't intimidate me."

"Wasn't tryin' to," he said. "Sorry ma'am. I just get worked up too quick these days. I care about Ernie and Joan. That's all. Didn't mean nothin' by it."

He took a step back and some of the tension went out of his big body.

"He's your buddy and she's his girl. I get it," she said. "But like Jimmy says, you need to know the truth. And so does your buddy, Ernie. Every guys needs to know how his girl acts when he ain't around. Especially if he's off fighting in a war for his country, protecting the very freedoms she's at home enjoying."

"So tell us about her," Orson said. "The straight scoop."

"Joan's not a bad girl, she ain't, but she don't exactly act like she belongs to anyone. You know how some guys are chasers? Well, some girls are . . . they make it known they're lookin' to be chased. She's always looking—and she had the look, you know the one? You could see it in her eyes. She was always looking for . . . something . . . someone . . . some kind of . . . thrill, like she was bored . . . or at least restless."

She paused. I nodded. Orson didn't overreact. She continued.

"Now, I've seen a lot of girls in my day," she said. "A lot. And I watch them. Tell the truth, I watch everyone. You two would be surprised at all I could tell you about yourselves. Of the girls like Joan there are the kind who act restless and look around, but without any real intention behind it. They flirt with the thrill, but that's it. They ain't about to run off with it and actually do anything. Then there's the ones who aren't satisfied 'til they're racin' headlong toward a cliff with someone snippin' the brake lines."

"Which is Joan?" I asked.

"I would've said the harmless flirter, but . . . now I'm just not so sure. She could've run off to be in pictures like she talked about. She could've run off with a man who promised her the moon. Shoot, she could've joined the circus. I just can't say for sure. And that's not like me."

"What about the guy who used to come in and just stare at her?" I said. "Lauren said you might know how we can find him."

"Somethin's surely not right about him," she said. "Never spoke a word—to anyone. Just sat and stared at Joan. I finally had to ask him to leave. When he wouldn't, I had a couple of the boys toss him. They had a bit of a scuffle outside—well, let's call it what it was, they beat him up. Said even during all that, he never said a word. He came back the next night, but hasn't been back since."

"Lauren thought that might have coincided with Joan's disappearance," I said.

"Oh, you know, it may just have. Wow. Do you think he could have . . . Oh my. One of the boys said they've seen him a few other places. I could get him to help you find him."

18

A GI named Otis took us around to the places he had seen the guy they all just called The Creeper.

Otis was average in every way—average height, average build, average intelligence. In his uniform and with his buzzcut, he looked like a hundred thousand other GIs.

We started at Nick's.

And ran into essentially the same crowd that had been there the night before—including Sweaty Neck and his friends.

They were shooting pool in the back room and worked real hard at not seeing us when we walked in.

Cab Callaway's "Blues in the Night" was on the Wurlitzer.

The dance floor was full.

The strong liquor was flowing.

The crowd was cacophonous.

While Otis looked around for The Creeper, Orson and I stood in between the bar and the dance floor and looked around a little ourselves.

"Being here bringing up any memories?" I asked.

He shrugged. "Maybe."

He then saw a woman at the bar, another working woman not unlike Betsy, though not as polished or professional.

He rushed over to her.

"Hey," he said. "Patricia, right?"

Her head reared back, her eyes flung open wide, and her mouth fell into an alarmed O. She looked genuinely frightened to see him.

She glanced from Orson over to me, to my missing arm, then back to him.

As if oblivious to her frightened reaction, Orson said, "You were here last night, weren't you?"

"I don't want no trouble, mister," she said. "Just leave me alone. Please."

The man sitting on the other side of her, a blond-haired, brown-eyed boy with red splotchy skin in an air force uniform, turned toward us.

"What is it, Patty?" he asked. "What's wrong? He bothering you?"

"I just want to ask you about last night," Orson said.

"Look, pal," the airman said. "She said she didn't want to talk to you, so beat it."

He then made the mistake of getting off his barstool and standing near Orson, who would have dwarfed him even if he had been standing on the barstool.

"I ain't gonna hurt you," Orson said to her.

"You're damn right you aren't," the airman said.

"Come on, Orca," I said. "She doesn't want to talk."

"But she was here. She can tell me what—"

"I saw you leave with Betsy," she said. "I know what you did."

People in our vicinity began to gather around us.

"Let's go, Orca," I said. "It's no good. She doesn't want to—"

"You killed her," she said.

"No, I—" Orson said.

"Who'd he kill, Patty?" the airman asked.

"Did you see me do it?" Orson said.

"Somebody call the cops," she said, louder now, nearly shouting. "He killed Betsy."

More people gathered around.

"No, stop," he said. "Don't do that. I just want to talk."

Someone unplugged the jukebox.

"What is it?" someone asked. "What's going on?"

"He beat her to death with his bare hands," Patty said.

Now the entire crowd had gathered around us.

"You like beating up girls?" the airman said. "Do you?"

He then grabbed a beer bottle from the bar and swung it at Orson's head.

Without taking his eyes off of Patty, Orson blocked the blow with one arm and swept the airman aside with it, tossing him several feet onto the dance floor and into the crowd.

"CALL THE COPS," Patty yelled. "HE'S A COLD-BLOODED SEX KILLER."

"No," Orson said. "It's not like that. I ain't like that. I just want to—"

"Orson, come on," I said. "We need to go. Now."

"KILLER," she yelled, feeding off the energy of the crowd quickly becoming a mob. "YOU'RE A KILLER."

"No," Orson said. "Stop it."

"KILLER. KILLER. KILLER."

In an instant he was on her, his huge body smashing her small one against the bar, his hands around her throat, his massive mitts enveloping her entire neck, throttling her.

"Stop it," he said. "Stop it. Stop saying that."

"ORSON," I yelled. "ORSON. STOP IT RIGHT NOW."

He didn't. He wouldn't. He was choking her, oblivious to me or the mob beginning to yell and swing at him.

Patty was trying to scream, but couldn't. She couldn't even breathe. Soon he would crush her windpipe and end her life.

"ORSON," I yelled again.

Still no response.

Withdrawing my revolver, I turned it over, grabbing the barrel and hit him a hard glancing blow with the butt of the gun on the back of the head.

He felt it, but twitched it off and kept killing her.

I hit him again.

And again.

Finally, he let go and turned toward the pain I was inflicting.

He started to grab me around the throat.

"Orca, it's me, Jimmy. Hey. Look at me."

He stopped, shook himself, and looked around as if having just regained consciousness or at least awareness.

"Jimmy?"

"Yeah."

"What're you—"

The circle around him opened up and Sweaty Neck charged him with a pool cue, popping him hard across the head with the fat end of the stick.

"This is for last—"

Orson hit the man with a backhanded fist, a single blow to the sweet spot on the side of his chin. His head snapped, a line of spit flew out the side of his mouth, and he went down hard and didn't get up.

The rematch between Orca and Sweaty Neck had gone just like the first—a one-punch knockout in the first round.

19

"You think he would've killed her?" Lauren asked.

"*I* do," Clip said.

I nodded.

We had cut the search for The Creeper short after the incident at Nick's. I had taken Orson home and put him under the care of his grandmother, dropped Otis off at the USO, and now Lauren, Miki, Clip, and I were having a late supper in the back corner booth at the Bird of Paradise.

The Bird of Paradise was Panama City's only queer club—and one of only a few places the four of us could go together and be both accepted and welcomed.

It was an old, small fishing shack on the end of a dock out in Massalina Bayou, marked by a large, iridescent Ribbon-tailed Astrapia painted on the front slat-board wall, its huge head and neck shimmering, glittering green and gold and blue, its full body a rainbow of brilliant colors on the tips of shiny black feathers.

This small fringe establishment was one of my favorite places in town, mostly because of its owner, Thomas Queen, who didn't ask but told us what we would be having every time we came to eat here––which was often, and often late at night.

It was late, but not late enough for the place to be busy yet. The perfect time.

Only a smattering of patrons were present—a few at the bar, a few around the jukebox, a couple in the booth in the opposite corner from ours. All homosexual men and women except for one heterosexual couple having an affair—something I knew because this was one of the places Lauren and I frequented back when she had a husband and we had to hide.

In his deep and smoky, soft and sensual voice, Tommy Q had said, "Honey, y'all will be havin' the very best grilled bay shrimp you ever put in your sweet little mouths. Now, I didn't say the best *thing* you ever put in your mouth, but I guaran-damn-tee it'll be the best shrimp you ever did. Those big ol' bay shrimp are just a marinating in my own special sauce. Well, not *my* sauce. Get your mind out of the gutter, Clipper Jones. I'm taken. And that, sugar is just the appetizer. Then for your entrée, I've put together the most delicious lump blue crab meat–covered filet of scamp imperial. With the most delightfully crisp white wine. How's that sound?"

"Divine," Lauren said.

"That'll do," he said. "Now, can I get y'all a little *cock*tail while you wait?"

Next to his deeply tanned skin, Tommy's bright white teeth and silver eyes sparkled brightly––the latter matching his coarse, closely cropped white hair.

"Is it just me or did he emphasize the *cock* in cocktail?" I said.

"It's just you," Tommy said. "Better keep your eye on this one, Lauren. He's hearin' emphasized cocks."

"No," she said. "I heard it too."

"Me too," Miki said.

"How about you, Clipper Jones? Did you hear me, ah, emphasize anything?"

"I shore as shit did not," he said.

"See?" Tommy said. "I rest my cock—I mean case."

Which is how we were sitting at the Bird of Paradise drinking cocktails and talking about our cases.

"So big whale kill hot pants hooker?" Miki said.

"He may just have," I said. "Don't know for sure yet."

"*I* do," Clip said. "You better get his ass in a cage. You don't and he do it again, we all know who you gonna blame."

"Yeah," I said. "Hitler."

"They do send some unexploded bombs back home tucked deep inside our boys, don't they?" Lauren said.

"That they do," I said. "I talked to him on the way home. He didn't remember much of anything. It's like he has these . . . envelopes of time. Can't see anything inside them."

Our wine and appetizer arrived, and we toasted and ate together like the great good friends and unlikely associates we were.

And it was good. Very good.

From behind the bar, Tommy said, "I'm not even gonna ask y'all if I was right, 'cause I know I am. Aren't I?"

We all nodded.

The door opened and Mama Cora ambled in, smoke from her long, ivory churchwarden pipe swirling about her big, beautiful head.

That's another reason this place was among my very favorites in town—the people who frequented it. Or as Tommy says, "freakwent" it.

Mama Cora was a three-hundred-pound, caramel-skinned Creole woman with closely cropped rust-colored hair that stayed mostly hidden beneath her colorful silk do-rag. As usual she was adorned with a plethora of rings—on her fingers and in her ears and nose.

She was the daughter of a French-African woman and a white

man and had traveled the world singing, and, when she was younger and smaller, dancing.

"Hello, soldier boy and friends," she said. "It is most agreeable to see your beautiful faces."

"And yours," Lauren said.

"We love Thomas's big bird, no? Everyone is welcome."

"We do," Lauren said, and we all nodded.

"Soldier, take a moment for Mama before you leave, okay? Needs must tell you a thing or two."

"Was planning to anyway," I said. "Have a question or two for you."

"Then we will have a meeting of the minds, no?"

I nodded.

"She is so very beautiful," Lauren said as she lumbered away.

"Perfection of skin," Miki said. "But not as pretty as Lady Boss Lauren."

Before I could second that sentiment, Clip said, "Not nearly as pretty as *you* and Lady Boss Lauren."

"Why, Clip," Lauren said. "That may by the sweetest thing you've ever said to me. Thank you."

We finished our shrimp and I awkwardly poured us another glass of wine.

"Would think you be better with that hand by now," Clip said. "Seein' how it the only one you got."

"Would, wouldn't you?"

"He's just fine with it," Lauren said. "Just fine."

Miki, who didn't have to be Judy in here, blushed.

"So, tell us about Gary and Rita before our food arrives," Lauren said.

"Well, first y'all do know they's lots of places a nigger and a Jap can't go," Clip said, "so we not the, ah, ideal team to be followin' white people 'round."

"Noted," I said.

"Judy here can pass in a pinch, but my black ass can't pass for shit—not even high yellow."

Judy smiled adoringly at Clip and bit her tongue to keep from jumping in and telling the story like she wanted to.

"But neither of them met anyone—least not at the places we could follow 'em. If they did in the places we couldn't follow, they only met a minute or so. Not long at all. It like she lookin' for someone, but can never find him. She just go from place to place, look, then leave. Just like at Nick's last night. They easy to follow tonight. All we had to do was follow her 'cause his ass was too."

"She go," Miki said. "He follow. We follow."

"Just go places, look, and leave—bars, soda shop, hotel lobbies, the beach. The Barn Dance."

"Go, look, leave," Miki said.

"Go, look, leave," Lauren said.

"What is she looking for?" I said.

"When you were following me," Lauren said, "I was looking for you."

20

While the others were finishing their scamp imperial, I slipped over to talk to Mama Cora.

"Mama been hearin' 'bout your troubles," she said.

"I thought nobody knew the troubles I seen but Jesus," I said.

She laughed, her fat cheeks pushing her eyes nearly closed.

"We will deal with that miserable Lady Bird Bennet and that wicked Noah Mosley, I assure you," she said of the two wealthy Bay County kingmakers and lever-pullers I had run afoul of on my last case, "but for now tell me about this friend of yours they say killed Betsy."

I did.

"There anything in it?" she asked. "Tell Mama the truth, you."

"I'm just not sure," I said. "I'm going to find out. The boy I knew, the man who left here to serve his country, could never have, but . . ."

"But the man they sent back?"

"He's the one I'm worried about."

She nodded and thought about it.

I looked back over at Lauren. She looked very tired.

Erwin, Tommy's partner of twenty years, arrived and joined Tommy behind the bar. The two men kissed affectionately, comfortably, companionably, the way Lauren and I do now, the way I hoped we would still be doing on our final day together—however close or far away that might be.

"Mama has information for you. You want it, you?"

"I want it, I."

"The word on the road is Betsy had a single john for a while, a wealthy older man who paid for exclusivity—something, it turns out, Betsy was not suited for. From what Mama hear he was most displeased. Perhaps he did something about it."

"That's very interesting," I said. "Thank you for that. Any idea who the man is?"

"Mama is working on a name for you," she said. "They were both very discreet, as you can imagine."

"Thank you," I said. "I really appreciate it."

"Mama trust you to do the right thing," she said. "Now, what was it you needed to consult with Mama about?"

"Sabotage," I said, and told her what Henry Folsom had told me.

"Is a good plan," she said. "Too much beach for spotters and patrols to cover. I will keep my eyes open and ears to the ground. We will stop them. You'll see, you."

DINNER WAS over and Lauren and I were dancing to one of our favorite songs, the song that, while we were apart, had been our song. Now that we were back together it resonated even more.

She was weak and I had to help hold her up, which with one arm was a challenge—a welcomed one I was grateful for. It was a grace to hold her, to dance together again—something neither of us thought we'd ever get to do.

I'll be seeing you

In all the old familiar places
That this heart of mine embraces
"People think we're silly," she said.
"They wouldn't if they knew."
In that small cafe
The park across the way
"What we've been through?" she asked. "What it has cost us to be together?"
"What it's like to have what we have and lose it," I said, "and then get it back."
She nodded. "That's exactly it," she said. "Think about how people would live, if they lost their lives, then got to come back and live them again."
"And it's not just us," I said, nodding toward the two other couples on the floor.
Clip and Miki were dancing every bit as intimately as we were. Tommy and Erwin even more so.
She turned to look.
Seeing Tommy and Erwin reminded me of Jeff Bennett and Kay Hudson and all those who for whatever reason couldn't or wouldn't express their love.
"We need to express our love for all those who can't or won't or don't dare to," I said.
"We certainly do."
I'll be seeing you
In every lovely summer's day
In everything that's light and gay
"That's us," Tommy said.
"Light in our loafers," Erwin said. "And gay as a picnic basket."
Everyone in the bar not dancing clapped and cheered for them.
I'll find you in the morning sun
And when the night is new

I'll be looking at the moon
But I'll be seeing you

"Take me to our home, put me in our bed, make love to me, then hold me while I sleep," Lauren said.

Without wasting any time, I did exactly that.

And we fell asleep entangled in each other beneath a waning moon as our song, one of our songs anyway, spun atop the phonograph.

And when the night is new
I'll be looking at the moon
But I'll be seeing you

21

"The things I'm seeing . . ." Dr. Robert Foster said. "The outer wounds—the bullet wounds, shrapnel, even missing limbs—" he glanced at my missing right— "are nothing compared to the mental, emotional, and psychological trauma they're dealing with. And nobody much is addressing those ailments at all."

Bob Foster was a physician in town who had a lot of GIs and other returning servicemen as patients. He was a thin middle-aged man of average height, with thick salt-and-pepper hair and an ill-advised bushy mustache above his thin lips.

We were having breakfast together at the Lighthouse Cafe, a milk bottle–looking joint located on the lower end of Harrison.

It was early—right in the heart of the morning rush, and Foster spoke softly because of the number of men in uniform close by.

I had left Lauren in bed, but carried her scent on my skin and our song in my head.

"You gotta remember we're fighting this war with essentially a civil army," he said. "These citizen soldiers aren't prepared for, equipped, or trained to deal with the horror, brutality, and inhumanity they're faced with over there—not that anyone ever really can be. But at least the professional soldiers undergo more extensive training—not to mention they have a certain disposition to begin with that a lot of the lads being drafted or even volunteering because of Pearl Harbor don't."

"The friend I mentioned to you is the least likely combatant you're likely to meet. He's kind and sensitive and quiet and—"

"Oh God," he said. "The worst. You couldn't design a better candidate for shell shock if you tried. How's he eating and sleeping?"

"I'm not sure."

"Does he seem keyed up, overstimulated? But also depressed and self-destructive? Is he more negative or hostile in general? Does he seem to find the world a more dangerous place—even in those places or times when it's not? Do certain things set him off, cause him to act in violent or aggressive ways?"

"I'd say yes to all, but haven't been around him much yet," I said. "I'll keep an eye out for those things."

"Find out what's in his nightmares," he said. "What here at home reminds him of what happened over there."

"Is it possible he could do things—violent acts, real bad things––and not remember?"

"Entirely. Absolutely. It's common, actually."

My appetite was gone. I pushed back my wrecked Adam and Eve on a raft and dropped my napkin on it.

"You need to keep a close eye on him," he added. "And feel free to bring him to see me. I can help."

WHEN I GOT to my office, Gary Thomas was there with a sweet, soft-spoken brunette named Betty Blackmon.

Betty was not only Gary and Rita's neighbor, but a good friend of Rita's and her coworker at the phone company.

"You don't think my wife is cheating on me," Gary said. "I brought proof."

"I never said your wife isn't cheating on you. I said there's no evidence that she is so far. And that's not proof, that's a person."

"I just meant . . . she can tell you since you won't believe me."

"Whatta you have to say for yourself?" I said.

Her eyes widened and she looked a little frightened. "Sir?" she asked, the hint of alarm in her voice. "I . . . I'm not sure I . . ."

"He just means tell him what you told me," Gary said.

"Rita's a friend of mine. One of my best, but . . . what she's doing . . ."

"And what exactly is that?" I asked.

"Well, seeing someone."

"Who?"

"I have no idea. She's very, very discreet. Obviously, they both are."

"Then how do you know?"

"She keeps slipping off when we're out together," she said. "She keeps lying to me and to Gary. I feel so bad about talking to you about her like this, but the way she's doing Gary, it's just . . . He's such a good husband and they used to be so happy. She's just come under this new guy's spell and I hate it for her."

"You've tried talking to her?" I asked.

She nodded. "She can't be reasoned with. She just says she can't explain it, but the heart wants what the heart wants."

"See?" Gary said. "Now will you please try to find out who she is seeing?"

"Yeah," I said, "because we weren't trying before."

22

Henry Folsom and David Howell showed up about lunchtime.

"You boys here to take me to luncheon?"

"Wish we were," Folsom said.

"We got another one," Howell said.

"Another what?"

"Body," Folsom said.

"Just like the other," Howell said. "Same place, same manner of death, same type of girl."

"Same killer," I said.

"What we hear," Howell said, "he nearly killed her inside Nick's earlier in the evening."

My throat constricted and I couldn't speak for a moment.

Folsom said, "Were you there when he choked Patricia Hightower? Patty?"

I frowned and nodded, still unable to say anything.

"Jimmy, I really don't want it to be him," Folsom said. "But . . . it certainly looks like it is. You've got to see that. You've got to see how careful and slow we're moving on this thing."

"Too slow," Howell said. "Cost another girl her life. If I had arrested him yesterday . . ."

"Witnesses say he left with you," Folsom said. "That true? Where'd you go?"

"I took him home," I said. "Told his grandmother how bad he was feeling. She said she'd keep an eye on him."

They both nodded as if I had just solved their case.

"Did someone see him back at the bar?" I asked.

"No, but—" Folsom said.

"With Patty?"

"No."

Howell added, "She left alone. We think she was jumped somewhere on the sidewalk and dragged into the lot. He was sore at her. Embarrassed. Upset. Out of his mind. He waited for her and when she came out, he got his revenge."

"How else can it be?" Folsom asked.

I shrugged.

"You wanna ride over with us to pick him up?"

Orson's grandmother answered the door in her nightgown.

"Jimmy? What's wrong?"

She squinted at us behind her glasses, the wrinkles on her old face multiplying.

"We need to talk to your grandson, ma'am," Folsom said.

"He's not here right now," she said.

Folsom and Howell looked at each other.

"What's this about?" she added.

"Where is he?" I asked.

"Out looking for Joan," she said. "I thought you were helping him."

"I am. But I haven't seen him since I dropped him off with you last night."

"What time did he leave again last night?" Howell asked.

"He didn't."

"But you said—"

"That he was gone now," she said. "He just left."

"You're saying he was here all night?"

She nodded. "I am."

"But he could've slipped out while you were asleep," Folsom said. "Right?"

"Wrong," she said. "I didn't sleep."

"You didn't sleep?"

"Not a wink. Why you think I'm in my bed clothes at this hour? I was just about to lie down when you showed up. I stayed up with Orson all night. I don't sleep so good anymore anyway, but when Jimmy told me he was upset and to keep an eye on him, that's exactly what I did."

"He was never out of your sight all night?" Howell asked.

"He was not."

"Ma'am, you can get in a lot of trouble for lying to the police," Folsom said.

"I'm not. I'm telling the truth. Have nothing to lie about. And I wouldn't if I did."

"Another girl is dead," Howell said. "If you're lying more could die. Can you live with that?"

"Won't have to. 'Cause my boy's not a killer and I'm not lying."

"Any idea where he is now?"

She shook her head. "None. Just know he's out looking for his best friend's girl. That's the kind of boy he is."

"Okay," Folsom said. "Have him call me at the station when he shows up."

"Jimmy," she said, "you know what a sweet boy my Orson is. Don't you let them go settin' him up for something he didn't do, something he could never do in a million years."

23

"I've learned a lot about her," Lauren said. "Far more than I would've thought I would. There's more to her than meets the eye."

"Yeah?"

Earlier in the day I had taken Lauren by Lilium Wynn's, Joan's aunt, where she had been allowed to look in Joan's room and through Joan's things, and from which she had taken Joan and Ernie's correspondence.

Knowing he was coming home soon, Ernie had mailed Joan's letters back when he was injured, so we had both sides of the ongoing wartime epistolary conversation.

"I feel guilty," she said. "Some of it is so intimate. I don't mean sexually, although there is some of that. Mostly I mean in the way they bare their souls to one another. It was certainly not meant for anyone else to ever see."

I nodded.

It was evening, and I was driving Lauren to the USO for her shift, our car rolling along Grace Avenue very slowly toward downtown.

"I've glanced over his, but the ones of hers I've read, I've read very carefully."

"And?"

"I feel so bad for her," she said. "I wish I had known her better, had been able to help her more. She's a really good person. Restless, like everybody's been saying. Kinda bored and sick of the small town. But mostly she's dangerously naive."

"That's never good," I said.

"But far worse in some circumstances than others," she said. "Boyfriend on a foreign battlefield, time on her hands, little to no supervision or even friendships."

I glanced over at Lauren. She was so beautiful, so my ideal woman, but she looked tired and frail, and I was glad we were going back to the doctor tomorrow.

"Don't forget we've got Dr. Reed in the morning," I said.

"I won't."

"I want you to be very honest with him about how you're feeling," I said. "And very detailed."

"Yes, sir."

"I mean it."

"I know you do. But back to Joan."

"Did she do anything besides volunteer at the USO?" I asked.

She shook her head. "One of the issues we're facing with the USO—and not just ours, but all of them—is only the well-to-do can work at them. Only we have the money and the time. Some of the women who would like to be able to, who would be very good at it, can't do it. In fact, many of them are domestics, working in the homes of those who are doing it, enabling them to."

A little flash of illumination went off inside my head.

"That's why you've employed a few maids who never actually come to our house to clean," I said. "You're paying them to volunteer at the USO."

A small smile played across her lips. "You notice everything, don't you?"

"God, I love you," I said. "And I love what you're doing with Harry's money."

"It's not Harry's money anymore," she said. "I keep telling you. It's our money. Yours as much as mine. I wish you would—"

"What else?"

"She genuinely cares for Ernie," she said. "She's not an Allotment Annie. She really loves him."

Allotment Annies were women who married men before they left for war in order to receive the allotments the military deducted from GI's paychecks. Some of the more unscrupulous Annies married several soldiers and were paid well for their bigamy. Of course, the big payoff came when their "husbands" were killed in action and they collected the ten grand paid to surviving wives.

"But?" I said.

"She loves him, but something changed. I'm not sure exactly when. I haven't gotten to all the letters—and most of them aren't dated so I'm having to establish their order by what's in them. But there's a definite change—and not too long ago, I'd say. It's a pretty subtle shift, but it's there. She doesn't get cold, but she definitely cools off. You know what it is? It's not so much that she grows distant as distracted. Something catches her eye, her attention."

I thought about it, what it might be, what it could mean.

"You think The Creeper took her?" she asked.

I shrugged. "Hope to find out tonight."

"The thing is . . . if she was taken, abducted, forced somewhere against her will, wouldn't you expect her letters to remain just the same, then stop abruptly? Doesn't the fact that she changes mean it's more likely that she chose to go off somewhere on her own?"

I nodded. "Yeah. That's good. Very good. Of course, both

could be true. She could've changed and even decided to go off somewhere or do something new, but before she could, she was taken."

"True."

"I think her being taken or something happening to her is the most likely because she hasn't contacted her aunt. Wouldn't the girl in the letters contact her aunt?"

"Yes, she would," she said. "She definitely would. So find the creepy bastard and get her back. Just be careful doing it. Make sure you come back to me tonight."

"I'll come back to you every night," I said. "Can I ask another favor?"

"Anything."

"Mama Cora mentioned Betsy had a single customer for a while—a wealthy, older, jealous john who didn't want to share her with anyone. She left him—"

"And you want to make sure he didn't retaliate," she said.

I nodded.

"And since I'm a woman of means . . ."

"Thought you might know who to ask—or even that someone might come to mind."

"You want it to be Noah Mosley, don't you?"

"Sure, but don't expect to be that lucky."

"You never know," she said. "From what I know of him, he could be the john."

"Don't tease me," I said. "It's cruel."

We pulled up in front of the USO, but before I got out to help her in, she said, "I'll see what I can find out. You just remember what I said. Stay safe and come home to me tonight so we can enjoy our favorite part of the day in our bed together."

24

Otis and I were back out looking for The Creeper.

Otis was looking as nondescript as ever—something I couldn't help but believe would work to our advantage.

It was a dark night—and cold, with gusts of wind that made you feel like you weren't in Florida.

Like the night before, we started at Nick's.

To my surprise, Orson was there. We found him outside about to go in.

I rushed over to him and grabbed him by the arm.

He spun around like he was going to hit me, then squinted and shook his head, recognition slowly registering on his huge face.

"Jimmy?" he said, looking confused.

"What're you doing here?" I said.

I pulled him a ways down the sidewalk, away from Nick's and the people going in and out. Well, actually, I pulled on his arm a little, and he began to follow me.

He shook his head again, as if trying to come out from under anesthesia.

Otis stood in front of us, facing the street, trying to block as much of us as he could.

"Huh? Whatta . . . you . . . Looking for Joan," he said. "And I wanted to apologize to the girl from last night. Patty."

"Apologize for what?" I asked.

"Whatever I did. You remember. I blacked out, but you said I—"

"She's dead, Orson," I said. "She was murdered last night. The cops think you did it."

"Did I?" he said.

"You don't remember?"

He shook his huge head.

There was something in his eyes, something I didn't recognize. I couldn't tell if it was the presence of something new or the absence of something that had been there before, but there was a definite difference.

"Your grandmother said you were home with her all night," I said.

"Was I?"

"You don't know?"

"If she says I was, I was."

"You don't need to be here," I said. "Come on."

I turned to Otis. "I'm gonna take him to the car. You take a quick look around and see if he's here, then meet us back at the car."

"Roger that," he said.

"What do you remember from last night?" I asked.

Orson and I were in the car waiting for Otis. Motor idling, heat on.

Orson was in the backseat—well, actually, Orson was taking up the entire backseat—and I was looking at him in the rearview mirror while also keeping an eye on the passersby and the entrance to Nick's.

"I'm not sure," he said. "I have bits and pieces swirling around my head. Can't say for sure what night they're from."

"Do you remember going off with a woman? Making love? Getting upset? Hitting her? Hurting anybody in any way?"

He shook his head.

Otis walked out of Nick's as a couple of cops were walking in.

"That worked out well," I said.

"Huh?" Orson said. "What's that?"

Otis opened the passenger side door and got in shaking his head. "Not in there tonight."

"But did you see who is?" I said.

"Cops?"

I nodded, put the car in gear, and pulled away from the curb.

"Where to?" I asked.

"Dixie Sherman," he said. "He goes to the bar in there a lot. But keep your eyes peeled. I've seen him just walking around downtown several times."

I drove over to the Dixie, searching the crowds along the sidewalks as I did.

Orson and I stayed in the car while Otis ran in to check. We repeated this same procedure at the Tennessee House, the Marie, the Ritz Theater, and a few dozen other places—all of which yielded the same results.

Now we were riding around downtown, just looking, not sure what else to do.

Orson was quiet in the backseat, and though he was looking out the window, he didn't seem to be looking for The Creeper so much as staring into the distance at something unseen to all but him.

I had slowed several times to ask Otis if a guy I saw matching The Creeper's description was him, but so far none had been.

It was getting late. Soon we would have to call it a night. I needed to pick up Lauren from the USO, take her home, get her to bed.

"Well, fellas," I said, "looks like that's all we can do for—"

"There he is!" Otis exclaimed.

25

I looked in the direction he was pointing, Orson stirring in the backseat for the first time since he got into the car.

There on the corner was a slight man in an army uniform getting into a Diamond Cab.

"You sure?" I said.

Orson started to open his door, though we were in traffic and moving.

"Stay put," I said. "We're gonna follow him. If he has her, we need to know where."

He let go of the door handle.

"I need you to not do anything until I tell you, okay big fella?"

He nodded.

"I mean it. It's important. Could mean the difference in getting Joan back or not. Okay?"

He nodded again, but didn't say anything.

The taxi pulled away from the curb and we followed.

North on Harrison out of downtown. West on 6th. Past Grace. North on Jenks.

When the cab finally stopped and The Creeper got out, it was at a small clapboard house on Jenks less than two blocks and one street over from where Lauren and I lived.

Orson grabbed for his door handle again.

"Orca, no. Wait."

He looked confused, but then stopped, considered me, and leaned back.

The Creeper, peering over his shoulder periodically, walked from the cab, through the gate, into the chain link fenced-in yard, and into the dark house.

The cab pulled away.

I sat there wishing Clip was here with me, but he wasn't. He was following Rita Thomas and I had no way of contacting him.

"I'm going to wait here," I said to Otis. "Keep an eye on things. Will you and Orson take the car back to my office? If Clip is there, send him back. If not, ask Miki to call David Howell or Henry Folsom and send them."

"Yeah, sure."

"You did good," I said. "Thank you very much."

"Happy to help, sir."

"I ain't goin' nowhere," Orson said from the backseat. "Not leaving without Ernie's girl."

"I really need you to go with Otis and get backup."

He shook his head.

"I'm all the backup you need, brother," he said.

"Orca, please. I need you to—"

"Save your breath, pal. I ain't budging."

I shook my head. "Okay," I said. "We'll wait here. Otis, send Clip back fast. If you can't find him, then Howell or Folsom."

"Will do," Otis said.

I thanked him again and climbed out of the car quietly.

Otis slid over in the seat and I gently and quietly closed the door.

Behind me, Orson noisily disembarked and slammed the door.

I looked back at the house. The one light that had been on went out. Was that because of the door slam?

"Go," I said, and Otis pulled away.

As I looked for any other signs that The Creeper had been alerted to our presence, I whispered to Orson, "We have to keep it down. Be as quiet as possible. Don't want him to know we're here."

"Sorry," he said.

On the left side of the house was an empty, overgrown lot. The properties were separated by a hedge—one sparse enough for us to see through fairly well.

"Let's go over there so we can see the front and back doors at the same time," I said.

Without waiting he began to lope in that direction.

"Wait," I said, but he didn't.

He moved through the undergrowth like it wasn't there.

I followed.

About halfway in, an unseen car over on 11th or Grace backfired and Orson lost it.

Yelling, screaming, crouching in a defensive position, Orson appeared to be back on the battlefield—which in his mind I was sure he was.

"Orca," I said. "It's—"

He turned, knocked me down, and ran off.

By the time I was on my feet again, Orson was ripping off The Creeper's front gate, slinging it into the street and advancing on the house.

Assuming The Creeper, who was a fairly small man, would go with flight instead of fight when he saw the size of Orca, I ran toward the back.

I could hear Orson breaking down the front door, cracking and splintering boards, and the bang of the door hitting the floor.

I expected to hear yells or shots being fired but there was

nothing—only the howling of the wind and the desultory sounds of traffic in the distance.

Across the way and around the back, lights from other houses began to blink on, people inside them beginning to stir.

More sounds from the house—but only those being made by my mad friend. It sounded like he was running from room to room busting up furniture and breaking up the place.

By the time I reached the back door, Orson was kicking it down.

"She ain't here, Serg," he said. "No one is. Clear the next?"

"No," I said. "Stand down. Await your next orders."

He seemed to relax a little.

"Yes, sir."

"Guard the back door," I said, "and keep an eye out for The Creeper."

"Yes, sir," he said.

He then saluted and stood at attention beside the now permanently open door.

I searched the house, fast at first, then slowly and methodically. Orson was right. No one was here. But someone had been. And not just The Creeper. There was blood in the bathroom and women's soiled and bloodied clothes in the back bedroom, which wasn't a bedroom at all, but a dungeon-like cell that had been someone's special kind of hell.

26

"Where'd the hell he'd go?" Folsom asked.

I shrugged.

"You saw him come in here? You're sure?"

I nodded.

"Then less than ten minutes later, y'all come in and he was gone."

"More like five."

"Okay boys," he said to a group of uniformed officers, "search the yard, under the house, the neighborhood. See if you can find him." He turns to Otis. "Give 'em the description again."

Otis stepped up and described The Creeper.

"Thanks. Now Otis, you go out to the car with Lieutenant Ponds and wait there for us with Orson, okay?"

"Yes, sir," Otis said, and almost saluted, then turned and marched out just behind the uniform cops.

That left me, Folsom, Howell, two other cops I didn't recognize, and the coroner, who was still unclear why he was here since there was no body.

"Let's have a better look around," Folsom said. "And remember, there's still a chance he could be hiding in here somewhere so be careful."

We had already searched the small house a few times, but he was right. We could've missed something.

We paired up and began a more thorough search of the little house. I was with Howell.

We started with what was obviously The Creeper's closet. It was in a small bedroom with only a bed and a single chest of drawers.

"Found some mail," Folsom yelled from the other room. "Our boy's name is Demetri Christopoulos."

"Let's see what's in your closet, Demetri," I said.

We shoved the clothes around some and took another look at the closet itself before more closely examining the clothes.

"Not much," Howell said.

The closet was small. There was nothing in it but a single rod and some clothes hanging from it. A pair of pants, two white shirts, and three uniforms—all from different branches of the military.

"Not a GI," Howell said. "Just pretending to be one."

"To get in the USO and blend in other places," I said.

While Howell went through the pockets, I stepped over to the chest of drawers and searched through it—a search that yielded exactly nothing. Of the five drawers, three were empty. One had socks and underwear, the other ties, handkerchiefs, and tiepins.

"Nothing," he said.

"Same here."

Though we had searched beneath the bed before, we did it again—this time taking it apart and completely moving it.

Nothing.

We walked into the other room where Folsom and the coroner were.

"I can't say for sure that it's human blood," the coroner was saying, "but I have no reason to doubt that it is."

The blood was concentrated around a wooden chair in the center of the room and a mattress in the back corner, but it was everywhere.

Several women's garments were strewn about, all soiled and blood-soaked.

Both the chair and the mattress had leather restraints, and a small tray on a stand between them held blood-covered surgical instruments.

"No way to tell how much blood is actually in here," the coroner said. "So much has soaked into the floorboards and materials, and I have no way of knowing how many different people have actually bled in here. So I can't say with any certainty if anyone died in here due to blood loss or anything else."

Folsom nodded.

Howell seemed transfixed on the blood-splattered objects.

"You okay?" I said.

"The things we saw over there," he said. "In the war. All the . . . and you come home and there are worse things here."

One of the other cops started yelling for Folsom from the kitchen.

He turned and headed in that direction. We all followed.

The kitchen was small and in disarray.

"Look," the taller of the two older men said. "Figure this is how he escaped."

They had removed an old wooden pie safe from the wall to reveal a passageway that led down under the house and into a small tunnel.

"Take a flashlight and see where it goes," Folsom said to the smaller man. "Keep your gun out. We want him alive but don't get yourself hurt over it."

The smaller man nodded, took off his coat, withdrew his weapon, and was handed a flashlight by his partner. Then without a word he entered the passageway.

"You stay here," Folsom said to his partner. "Keep talking to him, checking on him. We're gonna go out outside in the direction the tunnel is headed. Be waiting for him out there."

The taller cop nodded, crouched beside the opening, shone another flashlight inside, and started talking to his partner.

Folsom went out the back door and we followed.

The night seemed darker and colder than before, the wind more biting.

"Damn," Howell said.

"This is the kind of cold that wipes out orange groves," the coroner said.

We walked in the general direction the tunnel seemed to be heading and found the other end before the cop inside made it to it.

A dirt and leaf-covered board had been left beside the hole—both of which were inside a small clump of trees and underbrush.

The cop's flashlight beam could be seen dancing down in the hole.

"Demetri Christopoulos is a smart boy," Folsom said.

"And was prepared for this day," I said.

"Which means he probably has money and supplies somewhere," Howell said. "Maybe another house, even."

27

"Y ou think she's dead, don't you?" Lauren said.

"I think it's likely," I said.

Patrol cops were searching the city for Demetri Christopoulos.

Orson was being questioned by Folsom and Howell at the station.

Ernie was on his way home.

Joan was still missing.

Clip and Miki were keeping an eye on Gary and Rita Thomas —or were earlier. They were probably back home now in a warm bed of their own.

Lauren and I were in our warm bed on this cold night, wrapped up in each other again, enjoying our favorite time of day.

As it often did at the end of the day, a quote from Emerson came to mind.

Finish each day and be done with it. You have done what you could. Some blunders and absurdities no doubt crept in; forget them as soon as you can. Tomorrow is a new day. You shall begin it serenely and with too high a spirit to be encumbered with your old nonsense.

"Huh?" I said.

Lauren had said something I missed.

"You're thinking of the Emerson quote again, aren't you?"

I nodded.

"Say it for me."

I did.

"What I said was," she said, "why do you think she's dead?"

"He's a vicious, demented killer," I said. "And she was obviously in his crosshairs."

"But—"

"Wasn't finished."

"Sorry."

"She went missing and he stopped coming around when she did—like he knew she wouldn't be there, like he knew where she was."

"God, I hope you're wrong."

"Not as much as me," I said. "It's going to destroy Ernie."

"So very much suffering in the world," she said.

"It doesn't make you question the existence of God?"

"If anything could . . ."

Lauren had undergone a spiritual transformation when we were together the first time. It wasn't something I fully understood, but it wasn't something I doubted either. I had witnessed it, had watched the fruit of it blossom not only in her life but in our relationship.

"Love is stronger than suffering," she said. "Even stronger than death. God is love. I believe in love."

"I believe in you," I said. "In us."

"What are we if not expressions of that love?"

I smiled. She had me. "I can't argue that."

We fell asleep in love. We woke up in love.

The next morning I took her to the doctor, and when I got to my office, Ernie and Orson were waiting for me.

28

"Welcome home," I said.

Ernie, in uniform, an eyepatch on his right eye and bandage on his left hand, was standing in the reception area with Orson, Clip, and Miki nearby at her desk.

He was thinner now, and there was something in his remaining eye that hadn't been there before—perhaps pain and a bit of humility—but much of the former twinkle, intelligence, and kindness remained too.

"Look," Orson said, "Ahab and Orca together again."

Ernie and I embraced.

He felt bony and a just a bit brittle.

"Haven't seen you since you lost your right jab," he said. "Now all I have to look out for is your left hook."

"I'm afraid without a right jab to set it up, it's not much anymore."

"Who you kiddin'?" he said. "It never was."

We all had a good laugh at that.

"What's going on with your left?" I said, nodding toward the bandage on his left hand.

"Lost a few fingertips," he said.

I introduced them to Clip and Judy, and Ernie and Clip compared eyepatches.

"How long'd it take your vision to adjust?" Ernie asked. "I keep missing steps and walking into walls. And my depth perception is for shit."

"I'm still working on it," Clip said.

"How long ago'd you lose it?"

"Couple a years."

"So, not fast," Ernie said. "Damn."

"Ain't much that's fast in my experience," Clip said. "'Cept maybe a few certain types of cars and women."

We went into my office, leaving Clip to translate his last statements for Miki.

"You's always different, Jimmy," Ernie said when we were inside with the door closed.

"How's that?"

"Walk your own way, don't you?" he said. "Always have."

"I don't follow."

"A Negro partner and a Jap secretary."

"Clip's more than a partner," I said.

"That's what I'm saying. How many guys you know have a black best friend?"

"I thought we was his best friends," Orson said.

"Not anymore, pal," he said. "That was childhood. Jimmy's all grown up now. He's put away childish things. It's a good thing. I admire it. We've all got to do it."

Orca nodded. "Lots of time has passed. Lots has happened."

"Certainly has," I said.

"So a PI, huh?" Ernie said.

I nodded. "It's where cops who get shot go to die."

"Speaking of cops. Orca tells me they sweated him all night last night. What gives, pal? You know as well as I do Orca's not a killer whale. Can't you set 'em straight?"

"I've tried."

"Well try harder, brother. Can't let one of the Three Muske-teers be treated like that."

"What all has he told you?" I said.

"Doesn't matter. There's no way he did it. No way. Don't tell me they got part of your brain when they got your arm?"

I laughed.

"I've missed you, pal," I said. "I really have. Why don't I get Clip to drive Orca home so he can get some sleep and we can catch up? That okay with you, big fella?"

"I could use a few winks," he said. "Sure could at that."

"Then it's settled," Ernie said. "Boy, what I wouldn't do for a real Southern breakfast."

"Am I really gonna get some breakfast?" Ernie said.

He looked like he needed to eat. I couldn't remember him ever being so thin—not even as a boy.

"Or," he continued, "did you just do that to get rid of Orca so we could talk?"

Clip and Orson had just left. Ernie and I were still in my office.

"I'm gonna get you some breakfast—and fast, but first close the door, will you?" I said.

"It's like that, is it? Damn."

He closed the door and sat back down in one of the client chairs across my desk from me, holding his bandaged hand up, which he said helped with bleeding and throbbing.

"The cops like Orca for two murders," I said.

"Anything in it?"

"Not sure," I said. "Could be. Have you noticed how much he's changed?"

"Look, pal, the only thing that's changed is you, if you think ol' Orca murdered anybody."

"I'm not saying he did. I'm saying given what I've observed of him, his behavior since he's been back, it's at least a possibility."

"No way. Not Orca. But why don't you give me the goods and let me decide for myself."

I did.

"So he was the last one seen with the first victim and he choked the second one right there in front of everyone?"

I nodded.

"He ain't been right since they put that plate in his head, hasn't been the same. Still . . . it's gonna take a lot more than that to make me believe he killed a couple of working girls. What kind of PI are you? Can't you find out who really did it?"

"Not much of one," I said. "But I'm working on it. It and a few other things—including trying to find your girl."

The perplexed expression on his face formed a question. "Whatta you mean by that?"

"Orca didn't tell you?"

"Tell me what?"

"Sorry, Ernie. I thought you knew. She's missing. Orca's been looking for her. I've been helping. I thought you knew he was."

"I asked the big lug to look in on her when he got here and tell her I wouldn't be too far behind him, but . . ."

"He tried to do that but found her missing. He's been searching for her. I've been helping him the last few days."

"*Last few days.* How long's she been missing?"

"Week and a half."

"*A week and a half.* Oh my God. Her aunt has no idea where she is?"

I shook my head. "Where would she go?"

"Nowhere," he said. "Not without telling me, her aunt, her friends.

"But if she was gonna go somewhere . . ."

He didn't respond, just continued to shake his head and stare off into the distance.

Suddenly, he stood. "I've got to find her, got to go talk to her aunt. Jesus, Jimmy. What the hell? Missing. I just can't . . ."

"Sit back down for a minute," I said.

"Why? I need to go talk to—"

"There's more."

"*More?*" he said, dropping back into the chair. "What more?"

When he looked at me again, something in his eye had changed. The twinkle and intelligence had been replaced by something far more blunt, angry, even crazed. Orca wasn't the only one who had changed.

"Seems she was being watched by a creepy fella named Demetri."

"Whatta you mean 'watched'?"

"At the USO. He'd come in and just stare at her for hours until the mom and senior hostesses did something about it."

"You think he may have taken her?"

"Ernie, I need you to brace yourself. Take a breath and prepare yourself."

"For what? Oh, God, no. For what? Is she—"

"We found Demetri last night," I said.

"And? Did he have her? Was she—"

I told him the entire story—with the exception of how much blood there was in the house.

He didn't speak for a long moment, then, "So you think this dead man, Demetri, took my Joan and . . ."

"We don't know yet," I said. "It's possible he had nothing whatsoever to do with her disappearance."

"You're just saying that to try to give me hope."

"No I'm not. I wouldn't do that. I would never intentionally give you false hope. There are two promising pieces of evidence to indicate—"

"What? What are they?"

"The cops had her aunt look at the items of clothing found at

Demetri's house. She said none of it was Joan's. Said she was certain."

He nodded. "That's good, I guess. It's not concrete, but it's a little— What's the other? You said two."

"Joan's car," I said.

"What about it?"

"It's missing," I said. "To me that indicates it's more likely that she went off somewhere rather than being taken. If Demetri had snatched her, I think her car would've turned up by now, left wherever he took her. If he took her and her car, it would've been at his house. It wasn't. He's been using cabs. He doesn't have her car."

"Then maybe he doesn't have her," he said, "but if he doesn't, who does?"

29

W hen I opened my door to let Ernie out, Henry Folsom and David Howell were standing there, Miki behind them asking in frustration for them to take a seat and wait.

"Jimmy," Folsom said like he always did.

"Talk to you a minute?" Howell said.

"Sure," I said. "But from now on show more respect for my receptionist, Judy, or we're not gonna be as friendly anymore."

Miki smiled and bowed a little.

"Sorry, ma'am," Howell said. "Didn't mean any disrespect. We get goin' on a case and just get like a bulldog with a bone."

"Beg pardon, ma'am," Folsom said. "Won't happen again."

Pleased, she took their coats and hats and went to put them away.

As she did, I introduced Ernie to them and them to him.

"You might want to stick around for this," Folsom said to him. "It's about your big friend."

We all stepped back into my office.

As the three of them were deciding which two were going to

sit in the two client chairs in front of my desk, my door opened and Miki walked in with another chair from Clip's office.

"Thank you, Judy," I said.

"Yes, thank you, ma'am," Howell said as he took the chair.

"If Clip gets back before we're finished in here, please send him in," I said.

She nodded, bowed, and left the room, closing the door behind her.

"By the way," Folsom said. "Where *is* the big fella?"

"At home catching some sleep," I said. "What we hear, you boys went at him all night."

"Yet we're still at work today," Folsom said.

"It wasn't nearly all night," Howell said. "Didn't start 'til late and didn't go long. We showed him every respect, treated him like a friend of yours. You have my word on that."

I nodded. "Thanks."

"But let's be honest," Folsom said. "The big guy's not right. How much of it's from before and how much of it's the war?"

"All of it," I said. "It's all war."

That brought on a reflective moment of silence.

I felt real bad for Orson—worse because I didn't know what to do for him or how to help him. He was a good man who'd gotten a bad deal doing good things for a good cause. The injustice of it made me livid.

Eventually Ernie said, "You fellas mind telling me what you mean? I haven't seen Orca in a few weeks—and guess I haven't seen the kind of things you're talkin' about."

"Jimmy," Folsom said, "why don't we let him hear it from you?"

"It's shell shock," I said. "He's jumpy and paranoid, easily set off—by everything from a woman telling him to leave her alone to a car backfiring. He blacks out, has huge holes in his memory, truly can't remember important things. He's got anxiety, not sleeping well."

"And he's not thinking straight," Howell said. "His mind's a mess."

"I don't doubt any of that," Ernie said. "Hell, I probably got some of that goin' on too. But he ain't a killer. No, sir. Especially not of women. No way."

"No one wants to believe his pal is capable of—"

"Mine's not," Ernie said. "And what kind of pal would I be if I could think he was?"

I wondered if that was directed toward me. I decided it had to be and that he was right to do it. How could I believe my friend, the boy who cried at the thought of leaving behind a seagull with clipped wings, could kill anyone? Yet he had in the war, hadn't he? He had been good at it. Was it so hard to imagine him continuing to do it now that he was back home?

"Out of honor to his service and what I owe Jimmy," Folsom said, "we're giving him all the breaks—and then some, but . . . we can't ignore evidence. If he were anyone else, he'd be in one of our cells by now."

"His alibi is his grandmother," Howell said.

"There was plenty at the crime scene to make a reasonable person question whether or not it was him," I said.

"If we don't lock him up and he does it again . . ." Folsom said.

"How about this?" Ernie said. "We become his chaperones. Me and Jimmy. One of us with him all the time. Then when it happens again, you'll know it's not him."

"If he was in one of our cells and it happened again, we'd know it wasn't him," Howell said.

"But given what the guy is going through, my way is more humane—and he deserves that. And did long before he went over and fought bravely and valiantly for his country."

"Jimmy?" Folsom said.

I looked at Ernie.

"I'll do most of the watching," Ernie said. "We're gonna be looking for Joan anyway. I won't let him out of my sight unless you're watching him. We can do this. Come on. We owe him that much."

I nodded. "I may get Clip to help too—just to make sure—but somebody will be watching him twenty-four seven."

"I hope you realize what a favor this is, Jimmy," Folsom said.

Howell shook his head. "I don't think it's a favor at all. Be better for everyone—including him—to lock him up."

"I wouldn't do this for anyone else," Folsom added. "Don't make me regret it."

30

"Three things kept me alive over there," Ernie said.

We were eating breakfast at a small cafe that had recently sprung up on Harrison just down from our offices toward 6th Street.

"These," he said.

He withdrew a tattered paperback from his back pocket.

It was an Armed Services Edition of A.J. Cronin's *The Keys of the Kingdom.*

Armed Services Editions were compact paperback editions printed by the Council of Books in Wartime and distributed to servicemen serving overseas. Meant for both entertainment and education, the compact books, which fit nicely in cargo pockets, consisted of classics to contemporary bestsellers and everything in between—fiction, nonfiction, poetry, drama, short stories, essays. Their distinctive covers read "Armed Services Edition: This is the Complete Book—Not a Digest." The abridged versions read "Condensed for Wartime Reading," or "Slightly Condensed for Rapid Reading."

ASE's slogan was "Books are weapons in the war of ideas."

ASEs were printed on pulp magazine presses when they were not in use, for very little cost—about six cents per book.

These extremely popular books were read and reread, shared and swapped, ripped and torn into sections to accommodate two or more soldiers reading at the same time. A recent newspaper commented that "The hunger for these books, evidenced by the way they are read to tatters, is astounding even to the Army and Navy officers and the book-trade officials who conceived Editions for the Armed Services." And a sailor was heard to say "A man is out of uniform if one of them isn't sticking out of his hip pocket."

Ernie handed me the book and returned to his breakfast.

I caressed it gently.

"I heard Hitler has burned over a hundred million books," I said.

He shook his head and stopped eating for a moment. "You know, for some of the boys these were the first books they had cracked open since school."

I shook my head and something I had heard a while back came to mind. *The man who doesn't read good books has no advantage over the one who can't.* I wasn't sure who said it—had actually heard it attributed to a few different people—but it was as true as anything I'd heard in a long time.

He returned to his breakfast.

Ernie and I had always shared a love of reading and had connected through books. Before he went off to war, we swapped books back and forth the way he had the Armed Services Editions over there.

Books had saved my life too. More than once.

The Keys of the Kingdom was a particular favorite—one Lauren had given me and that we both loved.

"Couldn't count on letters over there," he said. "They rarely arrived—and never on time. Some of the ones I received arrived more than five months after they were written. So whatta you do when you're lonely? Scared? Bored? Worried? You read. All the boys had these. I went through dozens and dozens—maybe all there was. I'm not sure. I would've gone crazy without them. They are one of the reasons I'm here today."

I nodded, took one more look at the book, and handed it back to him.

He shook his head. "Want you to have it," he said.

"You sure?"

He nodded. "Brought it all the way back for you."

"Thanks, Ernie. I really—"

"You've already paid me back," he said. "I took one from your office."

"What'd you get?"

"Graham Greene," he said. "*The Power and the Glory*. You had two."

I smiled. "And another couple of copies at home."

"Then you still owe me," he said. "This one doesn't count."

I nodded my agreement. "So," I said, "that's one. What're the other two?"

"Other two wh—oh. Joan, of course. Her letters—when I would get them—kept me going like nothing else. Knowing she was here, waiting for me, missing me the way I was her. The things she wrote me, the way we shared our very souls through pen and paper . . ."

"We're gonna find her," I said.

I regretted saying it the moment it was out of my mouth.

"I know. I can feel it. It's gonna be all right."

I should've said *I'm going to do everything I can to find her* or something like it.

"It's gotta be," he said. "Why else would I be spared, make it back home from hell—if not to be with her?"

"What's the third?" I said.

"Orca," he said. "He literally saved my life a half dozen times. This last time, he saved several of us. We were pinned down at the far end of Betio Pier. Jap shore batteries were blasting hell out everything. Orca, the big, fearless lug, kept defying death and the big blasts of the enemy bombardment to organize and lead all of us over the long, open pier to the beach beyond. Then the crazy bastard got a flamethrower and demolitions and started blasting hell out of them, taking out several hostile installations single-handedly. Never seen anything like it. He's gonna get the Congressional Medal of Honor. Mom is organizing a parade and a celebration for him here."

I nodded.

"What? Should I get her to wait?"

I shrugged. Thought about it. Then said, "No. Don't have her wait. Let's just help him out of this jam before the celebration takes place."

"Then we better hurry," he said. "She's planning it for next week."

When I got back to the office, Clip had both Gary and Rita Thomas there with him.

I was surprised, but not shocked. Nothing Clip could do would shock me.

I was alone. Ernie had gone to keep an eye on Orson until the three of us met up later to follow up on some leads.

"What's going on?" I asked.

"Just waitin' on you so we can proceed," he said. "Could I get you all to step into my office?"

They nodded.

"Sure," I said.

"May, I, ah, Judy too come?" Miki asked.

"'Course," he said. "You's a big part of this, baby."

She beamed—an expression that always made her look even more Asian, an expression all the carefully applied makeup, the tilted-down hat, and large sunglasses were impotent against.

When we were all situated in Clip's mostly empty office, Gary said, "This seems highly irregular to me. What's all this about?"

He and Rita were seated next to each other in Clip's client

chairs, but weren't touching, looking at each other, or interacting in any way.

Besides the two client chairs, the only things left in Ray's old office were an old empty filing cabinet, a desk, and the chair behind it, in which Clip was now seated.

Miki and I were standing to the side.

"Hold on," Clip said. "Didn't think this all the way through."

He pushed back from his desk, stood, and ushered Miki into his chair.

She bowed and said, "Ariga—thank you."

"So," Clip said, "I is broken the case wide open like I's some Negro Sherlock Holmes."

I smiled—as I often did at Clip. I could tell by the way he was talkin', the shift in his dialect, the attitude and tone of his bearing, that this was going to be entertaining if nothing else.

"I Jap Watson doctor," Miki said.

I actually laughed out loud.

"Is this some kind of joke?" Gary said, turning to look at me.

"I is no joke," Clip said.

"He is no joke," I said.

"I's a private eye with only one eye, but by God it's a good eye. When Jimmy put me in charge of this case—"

Something I wasn't aware I had done.

"—I pay close attention with this one eye. And Judy's two good one's a 'course. I know people. 'Specially women. And after just a little while of following Miss Rita here around—"

"You've been following me?" Rita said, shock and outrage in her voice.

"Your little mister there thought you's cheatin' on him."

"*Me?*" she said.

"Exactly," Clip said. "I could tell right away you's not cheatin' on nobody."

"I most certainly am not," she said.

"But to be absolutely certain," he said, "I gave you the Clip test."

"The Clip test?" I said.

"Yeah," he said. "I propositioned her. The Clip test. She able to resist me, she faithful as the day is long."

"Oh yeah?" Gary said. "Well, what about her nights? Her long nights when she's not at home, when she leaves her friend, what about then?"

"Ah yes, the friend," Clip said. "Or is she? Sweet, little, soft-spoken Betty Blackmon. I aks myself why you wandering around the city lookin' for someone you never find. Hell, if you was meetin' someone you'd a done met 'em by now. No, you's out on a wild goose chase."

"I was out lookin' for my husband," she said.

"And why?" Clip asked. "'Cause your good friend and neighbor Betty put you up to it. 'Cause she told you she'd seen Gary with another woman, right? Cause she told you some of the places he takes her and give you a supposed alibi while you goes and looks at them for Gary and this girl the bitch made up."

"Hey," Gary said. "I'll not have you talk about Betty that way."

"All the while she cozyin' up to ol' Gary, tellin' him she's seen you with another man, that she hears you talking to him at work, that she's even seen him over at your house. She drivin' him crazy with all this shit, all the while cozyin' up to him, gettin' ready to take your place."

A born entertainer, he paused for dramatic effect.

"Aks me how I know all this," Clip said.

"How do you know all this?" I asked.

"'Cause when my good eye saw what it saw, Negro Holmes and Jap Watson began to investigate sweet little Betty Blackmon. We follow her. We watch her. We read the notes she be leavin' for these two and see—"

"Through fake sweet," Miki said.

"So he's not cheatin' on me?" Rita asked me.

"Ask Negro Holmes."

She looked at Clip.

He shook his head. "No, he not."

"And she's not cheatin' on me?" Gary said.

"No, she not," Clip said.

"And Betty is . . ."

"The devil," Miki said.

"Case closed," Clip said. "Marriage saved. Detective legend born."

"I'm sorry I thought you were . . ." Rita said to Gary.

"Me too."

"Great work," I said. "You two make a great team."

"It elementary," Clip said. "All we do is . . ." He looked at Miki.

"Cut through white bitch's bullshit," she said.

32

E arly Evening.
A plumb-colored horizon had faded to black and now lightning was flickering atop the pines.

I was driving Lauren to the USO for her shift.

On our way, I cut over to Jenks and we drove by Demetri's place.

David Howell was in the yard, watching as uniform cops and the coroner worked beneath the house. He stepped out into the road when we pulled up.

As usual, he tried not to show any awkwardness in his movements, and, as usual, there were none—unless you knew what to look for.

"House belonged to a little old lady," he said. "Martha Westerton. Our boy slit her throat and threw her under the house."

"Oh no," Lauren said. "Poor thing."

"So maybe the blood was hers," I said.

"Some of it at least, I'd say. He had stuff hidden in the walls, under the house. Gonna take a while to go through it all. Hell, we haven't even found it all yet. There's a shed out back we haven't even started going through yet. But it looks like he might be a Nazi spy of some kind."

"*Really*?" Lauren said.

"It's at least a possibility," he said.

I nodded.

"Where is Orson?" he asked. "Thought you weren't going to let him out of your sight?"

"Ernie's with him now," I said. "I'll be with him in a little while. One of us will be with him at all times."

"That's an awful lot of trust Folsom's givin' you," he said.

"I've earned it," I said.

"Never seen anything like it. Just be careful. I still like Orson for it. Make sure he doesn't do it again."

"What if he didn't do it before?" Lauren said.

"I hope that's the case, but . . . I just don't think it is. I want to. I just don't."

"I understand," I said. "We should know one way or another soon. Please keep me posted on what you find here—and if there's any sign of Joan Wynn."

"Only if you keep me posted on what happens with the big fella."

"It's a deal," I said, and we drove away.

ORCA AND ERNIE met me at the USO and the three of us met with a girl named Linda Sue Sanger out in back by the bay.

Lightning continued to flicker in the distance but there was nothing in it. No rain. No thunder. Just a light show in the otherwise dark night sky.

The black night was biting, especially the breeze blowing in off the bay, but it didn't seem to bother anyone, including Linda Sue.

"Gee mister," she said, "I feel funny sayin' stuff to you about her if she was your girl."

"*If?*" Ernie said. "You didn't know she was my girl?"

"See? Like that. No matter what I say you'll be sore."

"We've got to have it," I said. "No matter what it is. Finding her is all that matters. Not his feelings. He wants to hear the truth."

She looked at him.

He nodded.

The night was so dark, especially with the wartime blackout, that the only evidence of the bay beside us was the undulating waters and their rhythmic splash against pilings, cement seawalls, and boat hulls.

"Why not just get it from the big fella?" she said, nodding to the enormous dark mass that was Orca.

He had yet to utter a word, just stood quietly in the darkness —listening, I assumed. I couldn't see his face.

"I've told it all to him," she said.

"You have?" I said.

"You have?" Orson said. "I don't remember."

"When?" I asked.

She shrugged—something I had an impression of rather than actually seeing. "A week ago," she said. "Maybe a little more. Wasn't long after she disappeared."

"I . . ." Orson started.

"You've talked to her before?" Ernie said.

"If I did I don't remember."

"It was right inside there," she said. "Told me you's looking for her for your buddy. Said you had to find her and fast."

"I . . ." Orson said. "I . . . don't . . . I can't remember."

"Just tell us," I said.

"Every word of it," Ernie added.

"I didn't mean she wasn't your girl or nothin', just that . . . well, Joan didn't seem like anybody's girl. No, that's not it. She seemed like everybody's girl. You know the type. Not in a bad way. I don't mean it as a bad thing."

"She said that's the role she was playing here," Ernie said.

"I'm sure it was," she said. "She was quite the actress. Everything was a part for her. She was meant for the stage or screen. She was frustrated she wasn't on either."

"We were gonna do something about that after I got home," Ernie said.

"See? She told me that. Said her fella was gonna make her a star."

"So why didn't you think she was my girl?" Ernie said.

"It's nothin' really. It's just . . . she was always sayin' stuff like that. That's what made me suspicious about those other guys. The ones I told Lauren about. She said they were going to make her a star."

"How? What guys?" Ernie said.

"I don't know. If she said their names I forgot, but she probably didn't 'cause she didn't want any competition. I'd like to be in pictures too. You know? Who wouldn't? She said one was a location scout and the other was a casting agent. Said they were real live Hollywood producers. Said they had worked on a picture shot in the Okefenokee Swamp near Waycross, Georgia a few years back. Said they discovered her as she was coming out of Walgreen's and they were coming out of the Marie Hotel. I just had a hard time believing it. Discovered her from across the street? I don't know . . . But I told Lauren and the big fella here because it was right about the time that she went missing."

"Did she say anything else?" I said. "Anything about them? What they looked like? Wore? The way they talked? Anything? Anything about the picture? The title? Director? What kind of film it was going to be?"

"Let me think," she said, raising her fingers to her mouth and chin. "What . . . else . . . did . . . she . . ."

"Jimmy," a voice out of the darkness yelled. "You down here?"

It was Clip's voice, disembodied in the darkness.

"Clip," I said toward the sound of his voice. "Smile so I can see you."

I heard Miki laugh, but I still couldn't see either of them.

"Howell just called the office," Clip said. "They found all kind a spy shit and explosives in Demetri's house and shed. He's a part of the Nazi sabotage plot."

We began walking toward them and soon they emerged from the darkness in front of us.

"They plan to blow up a train, some ships at the naval section base and Wainwright shipyard, some planes at Tyndall, the Dixie Sherman, and the USO when it's full. He thinks it's all gonna happen tonight."

33

"Lauren's in there," I said.

"Let's get her out," Clip said. "Others too."

Linda Sue started to scream and run away. Orca meant to put his hand over her mouth but it covered her entire face. He held her in place with seemingly no effort at all.

Miki said, "Calm down. Take breath."

She nodded and complied—perhaps moments before Miki was going to slap her.

"We gotta get in there," Orca said.

"What if they're watching? Ernie said.

"We've got to be quiet about it," I said.

"Cops are scrambling to the other targets," Clip said. "Howell asked us to see what we could do here. Sending backup when he can."

"We go in and get the civilians out," Orson said. "Then we deal with the Nazi bastards."

"If it's wired, we run the risk of triggering it or causing them to if we start a mass exit," Ernie said. "We could also start a panic and get people hurt—maybe for nothing."

"Be suspicious if Clip or Miki go in," I said. "Y'all take a careful and covert look around the outside while the three of us go in."

"How about panicky here?" Clip said.

"Look at me," I said to Linda Sue, my eyes locking on to hers. "You could get a lot of people killed if you don't calm down and—"

She mumbled something beneath Orca's mitt. He slowly moved his hand.

"I'm good now," she said. "Sorry I . . . reacted like that. How can I help?"

"She can stick with us," Clip said. "I'll keep an eye on her."

"Just one?" Miki asked.

"All I can spare," he said, and he and Ernie both laughed at that.

Orca turned and started running toward the front of the building.

"Whoa, big fella," Ernie said.

Orca slowed.

"Hey," I said. "We have to walk in there like nothing unusual's going on."

"Oh, yeah," he said, matching our pace. "Sorry, I forgot."

"We're just three pals out for a good time," Ernie said. "Talk to some pretty girls, eat some good food, take a twirl around the dance floor. Don't forget. It's important."

"Got it."

We slowly walked around to the front of the building, putting a hand on Orca occasionally to slow him down a little, all the while scanning the area for Demetri or anyone who looked suspicious.

Inside, I searched for Lauren while they looked for Demetri.

"Paper Doll" by the Mills Brothers was playing. The dance floor was full.

I'm gonna buy a paper doll that I can call my own

A doll that other fellows cannot steal

Servicemen and junior hostesses sat at tables talking. Senior hostesses were restocking trays with cookies and bowls with punch.

I'd rather have a paper doll to call my own

Than have a fickle-minded real live girl

I had always thought "Paper Doll" was sort of sad and pathetic. Johnny S. Black, a pianist who supplemented his income by boxing, had written it after being jilted by his girlfriend.

I spotted Otis dancing with a thin redheaded junior hostess. Weaving in and out of the couples, I crossed the dance floor to him.

"Hiya Jimmy. You cuttin' in?"

"You haven't seen The Creeper, have you?"

"*NO*," he said a little too loudly. "You think he's— He wouldn't come back here, would he?"

"What about anybody who's not quite right?" I said. "Somebody like him?"

"No, don't think so. Want me to look around?"

"Very discreetly," I said. "You can't be obvious about it. Can't look like you're doing it. Just dance and go get a drink or snack and casually, disinterestedly glance around. If you see The Creeper or anyone like him, don't make eye contact. Just come get me."

"Got it."

"Have you seen Lauren?"

"Try the kitchen or the storage closet. Think she was headed for one of them last time I saw her."

"Thanks," I said. "Remember. Be discreet."

After checking the kitchen and not finding Lauren, I went to the storage room.

She was hunched over something, her back to me.

"I'm so glad you're not a paper doll," I said.

She slowly turned toward me. I could see that what she had been hunched over was three large crates of Nazi rail buster dynamite. The crates were filled with sticks and sticks of dynamite, each wooden box bearing the official symbol of the Nazi party, the black eagle above a swastika.

34

Her mouth was taped shut and she was holding a grenade in each hand, carefully, the way someone would after the pins had been pulled.

The grenades were attached to the crates by cables, short leashes tethering her to the explosives and the reason for her being hunched over the boxes.

I stepped over, removed the tape, and kissed her.

"Where is he?" I asked.

"There were two. One held a knife to Mary Pat's throat and threatened to kill her if I didn't take what the other was handing me. He put them in my hands and pulled the pins. The other guy then killed Mary Pat anyway."

I followed her gaze over to the corner of the room where the lifeless body of a young woman lay crumpled.

"As they were leaving, he said they were going to light the fuse from underneath anyway so I shouldn't worry about being brave or heroic in trying not to let go. They've been gone about five minutes."

I took a minute to study the explosives.

The cables were welded to the grenades in Lauren's hands

and to the pins of other grenades built into the box and surrounded by the dynamite. I could see no way of unhooking any of the grenades without causing the entire contraption to explode.

"We're gonna figure this out," I said. "You okay? Just hang in there a little while longer."

"I love you," she said.

I stopped and looked at her, locking eyes. "I love you," I said. "Now let's get this figured out so we can get home and enjoy our favorite time of day together."

She teared up. "Sounds . . . good. Too good."

"Hey. Look at me. I'm gonna figure this out. Okay?"

She nodded, but her eyes and expression said she wasn't so sure. "We've been on borrowed time. We knew that."

The door opened and Otis walked in with Ernie and Orca.

"Jesus," Otis said. "What the—"

"Otis," I said. "Without causing a panic, I need you to get everyone to exit the building. Send them away. Tell them there's a water leak and we're closing up for tonight. Can you do that?"

"Yes, sir."

"But before you do that, I need you to check in with Clip. Tell him to make sure the bastards who did this aren't under the building lighting the fuse. See if he needs help. Tell him to come in when he can."

"Roger that."

He rushed out of the room.

Ernie was over by Lauren, studying the explosive device and introducing himself.

"I'm Jimmy's friend, Ernie," he said. "I hate to say it, but . . . you're way too pretty for him."

Orca hadn't moved, just stood staring that thousand-yard stare of his.

"You okay, big fella?" I said. "Explosives bringing back bad memories?"

"Fuckin' Nazis," he said. "I'd like to choke the life out of each and every one of them with my own mitts."

His words and the look on his face made me wonder which was more explosive—him or the dynamite?

"Let me confer with this lucky man that you're too good for over here for a minute," Ernie was saying to Lauren. "We'll be back with you in just a moment."

He stepped over to me and we both took a few steps out of the room.

He lowered his voice and said, "Jimmy, I don't see any way to disarm it or disengage her from it."

I nodded. I had come to the same conclusion.

"We could see where the nearest bomb squad unit is and get them over here ASAP, but I bet there's not one close, and I'm not sure there's anything they can do."

I nodded. I wanted to switch out with her, but lacked the necessary number of hands to be able to.

"I'm not sure how long she can hold out," I said. "She's very weak."

Clip walked up holding a gun on two bruised and bloodied men, both of whom had their hands tied behind their backs, Miki trailing not far behind.

"Found these two under the building trying to light the fuse," he said. "Talked 'em out of it."

"Let's check with Lauren to see if it's—"

"Jimmy!" Lauren yelled.

I turned to see her standing not far from me, empty handed. Behind her, through the doorway, Orson was now holding the grenades. At least I assumed he was. Nothing was actually visible inside his huge clenched fists.

35

"Orca!" Ernie yelled, stepping back into the small room.

"What're you doing?" I said as I embraced Lauren with my arm.

"That's them," she said, as she saw the two men Clip had.

"Don't let go, big fella," Ernie said.

"I ain't gonna let go."

Clip pulled back the hammer on his large revolver and pressed it to the back of the head of the guy nearest his gun hand. "How do we disarm it?"

The guy shook his head. "There is no disarming it. That's the beauty of—"

Clip pulled the trigger and the guy folded onto the floor.

Screams came from the exiting servicemen and hostesses.

Orson flinched and for a moment I thought he was going to lose it and destroy us all.

"Stay with me, big fella," Ernie said. "Right here, soldier. That's it. On me. My eyes. Right now."

Clip thumbed back the hammer again and jammed it into the back of the other guy's head. "How do we disarm it?"

"It really *is* impossible. But don't shoot."

"Okay," Clip said, then shot him too.

"Everybody clear out," Orson yelled. "Get everybody back to a safe distance."

"Orca, no," Ernie said. "You can't—"

"Now," he yelled. "I've got a plan."

"Share it with us," I said.

"I'm gonna carry these boxes down to the bay, drop them in, and duck behind the seawall. Worse that happens is I sleep the big sleep with some fishes, but who knows, maybe all I do is get us a mess of fish for a welcome home fish fry. Now get everybody as far away as possible."

"You can't carry all three boxes with your hands wrapped around the grenades," I said.

"Jimmy and I will help you carry them down to the bay."

"Shee-it," Clip said. "Jimmy got one arm and it about useless. I'll help carry the boxes."

"Long as you don't decide to shoot us on the way," Ernie said.

"Is it okay for me to say in this moment I'm glad you only have one arm?" Lauren whispered to me.

"You can," I said, "but I feel guilty enough as it is, and there's no way I'm not helping them."

"Whatta you mean?"

"They'll need an extra hand and I happen to have one. Clip and Ernie have two eyes between them. Orca could explode at any minute. They'll need help seeing, moving, watching. They'll need someone to help guide them, make sure no one stumbles or falls—or to catch them if they do."

"Why does it have to be you?"

"You know why."

"Yeah, I guess I do."

～

THE CROWDS HAD BEEN CLEARED BACK. The end of Harrison was empty.

Lauren, Miki, Otis, and others had backed those who hung around to a safe distance away behind other buildings down the street.

Ernie, Orca, Clip, and I were slowly making our way toward the bay.

It was dark and cold and quiet. The whistling wind, the undulating water, the clanging of rigging, a foghorn in the deep distance.

Lightning continued to flicker along the horizon intermittently, but it lacked intensity and provided very little illumination.

I was leading, my arm steadying Orson, who was carefully backing up in baby steps. Clip was on his left side carrying two of the boxes, Ernie on his right with one.

We all moved in unison, as if part of a carefully choreographed routine.

To ensure the cables didn't get too far apart and pull the pins, Clip and Ernie actually held the boxes up next to Orson, the wood pressed against the sides of his arms, maintaining constant contact to keep our world from ending.

It was slow going. We were about halfway between the building and the bay—which had taken quite a while.

"Least we saved the USO," Orson said.

"Actually, if it went off now," Ernie said, "it'd still do a lot of damage."

"Oh."

The ground was rough and uneven, our steps awkward and halting.

Orca stumbled several times. Each time, we stopped and I tried to steady him again. Each time, I realized if he started to fall there was no way I could keep him up.

We had only walked a few yards past the halfway mark when

an enormous explosion on the other side of the bay lit up the dark night sky, its fiery red and orange and blue flames shimmering on the water's surface multiplying the already massive explosion.

Expansive, breathtaking, and beautiful, it didn't look like what it was, didn't appear to be something related to sabotage, destruction, and devastation.

Ernie said, "Was that the shipyard or the naval section base?"

"Can't tell," I said.

"That a big fuckin' blast," Clip said. "Not sure the current plan be adequate enough."

"No way to know if the explosives over there are the same in kind or amount as these," Ernie said. "But, yeah, you're right. If they are, the seawall will be no match for the force and we'll be pulverized."

"Not *we*," Orson said. "*Me*."

"No, it's we," Ernie said.

"It's we," I said.

"Sound like they not gonna let you die alone," Clip said with a big smile. "I'll make sure everybody know what heroes y'all all was."

Everyone laughed.

"Would y'all feel the same way if you knew I killed them girls?"

"You didn't," Ernie said. "No way. I know it."

"I'm serious," Orson said. "No need for us all to die. Jimmy's got Lauren. He's happy. Doin' well. Clip has Judy. You've got to find Joan. Be a waste for us all to buy it."

"How about a boat?" I said. "We speed out into the bay. Jam the throttle. We jump overboard. Let the boat carry the explosives away from us for another five seconds or so."

"It'd still get us," Ernie said. "Bits of the hull would be like bullets piercing us. But . . . you know what might work . . . if we drop the explosives and we keep racing away. The water will help lessen the force of the blow. More so if we weigh the boxes down even more so they sink faster."

"Too bad we ain't got no boat," Clip said.

"Lauren!" I yelled into the darkness.

She was so far away I wasn't sure she would be able to hear me.

"LAUREN."

"YEAH?"

"WE NEED YOU TO BUY US A BOAT. FAST AS YOU CAN."

36

We had a boat.

Actually, we had two.

Wide, wooden bay bateaus used mainly for scalloping and oystering.

Ernie and Orca were in one.

Clip and I were in the other.

Miki and Lauren were with the others on land

The plan was the same—with Ernie driving fast, Orca would drop the boxes over the side along with the grenades he was holding and they would get as far away as they could before the explosion.

If the explosion capsized their boat or they had any other issues or injuries, Clip and I would be nearby in the other boat to pick them up.

"Thanks for the boats, baby," I called.

"My pleasure."

"I'd feel a lot better if y'all'd back up to where you were," I said.

"I'd feel better if you'd let me go with you," Lauren said.

"Mean that much to you," Clip said, "you can have my spot."

"I'll see you soon," I said.

"You better. Why not wait here until after the explosion?" she said. "Wait and see if they even need help."

"We've got to be close enough to be able to help," I said. "And we've got to stay close enough to be able to find them fast. It's gonna be hard enough to see as it is."

"Jimmy, you ready?" Ernie yelled.

"Anchors away, Ahab. You and Orca just—"

Just then another explosion lit up the night sky across from us, fire raining down like phosphorescent kite tails cut loose to ripple down into the roiling waters of the bay below.

As with the previous one, it was difficult to pinpoint where it had come from exactly, but it too was in the vicinity of the naval section base and Wainwright shipyard.

"We need to do this now," Ernie said.

"Right behind you," I said. "Let's go."

We both gunned the throttles of the old outboard motors and took off, the bows of our boats rising as we did.

The bay was choppy and the boats bounced about even at full speed.

We weren't supposed to have lights on because of the blackout, but both boats had running lights and handheld lamps with stronger beams.

With only one arm, I found it extremely difficult to throttle and steer the motor and use the handheld lamp. Seeing me struggle to do both, Clip crawled back and took the lamp. While he was moving back to the front, I used their running lights to follow them.

As we had planned, I slowed and let the distance between us increase.

Approaching the spot where we had discussed letting the balloon go up, I turned the throttle all the way down. Clip, back in the front now, lifted the lamp and we watched as they proceeded to execute the plan.

Our boat was rocking and it was hard to keep the light on them as it moved up and down and drifted around, but I could see Orca begin to stand and prepare.

Lifting the boxes.

Stumbling to the side.

Lightning flickering, the boat bouncing, salty water spraying up and into the boat.

Tossing the boxes overboard, the tethered grenades sailing through the air behind them.

One-one-thousand.

Orson falling back, as Ernie cranked down on the throttle.

Two-one-thousand.

Ernie reaching a hand up, grabbing Orca, pulling him down.

Three-one-thousand.

The boat bouncing as it sped away, looking like it might flip at any minute.

Four-one-thousand.

And then the blast.

A muffled *boom*, a huge waterspout shooting up, appearing to touch the tips of the fingers of light flickering above it, water like rain from a flash flood falling all around.

Ernie and Orcas's boat being lifted, back end aloft, end over end, the two men thrown from the small capsized craft.

Clip shining the lamp where they went into the water. Me gunning the throttle. Racing toward them.

Wave from the blast heading toward us, picking up steam.

Come on. Don't flip.

We hit the wave hard, its spray soaking us, the boat, and its contents.

The small vessel seemed to buckle, but it didn't break, didn't turn over, and we continued.

Judging we were close to where they went in and not wanting to hit them, I let off the throttle.

With the lamp, Clip located the capsized boat in a small debris field.

Standing, he scanned the area with the beam, searching both near the boat and farther away across the dark waters of the bay, but there was no sign of them.

I yelled for them as Clip continued to sweep the area with the lamp light.

Had we come to the wrong spot? Had they been knocked unconscious? Had I hit them with our boat? Were they drowning right now?

Had they survived the war only to come back and die a heroic death at home?

I kept yelling. Clip kept moving the beam about on the dark surface of the water.

Lauren yelled something from the shore, but she was too far away for me to be able to make it out.

Did she see them? Was she trying to tell us?

There was no way she could. It was too dark. More likely she was asking after us.

"I got the light, but can't see shit," Clip said. "You lookin' where I'm pointing it, case I miss 'em?"

I hadn't been, but I began to.

"Am now," I said.

I followed the beam closely as it played about the surface of the bay, but it wasn't until the lightning flickered again that we saw them.

There in the distance, blood on his huge head, Orca was treading water, holding an unconscious Ernie up to keep him from drowning.

37

"How you fellas doin'?" I asked. "You okay?"

I had stuck my head in the lost-and-found closet where Ernie and Orca were drying off and looking for some dry clothes to put on.

The chances of Orson finding anything that would fit were minuscule, but he searched through the boxes like that wasn't the case.

"Head aches," Ernie said. "Feels like Glenn Miller's got his entire orchestra set up in there playing their biggest, most dramatic tunes. And my ears are ringing."

"How about you, big fella?"

"Swell," he said. "Just peachy, pal. And what he said."

"Orca's a hero again," Ernie said.

"You both are."

"Saved my life," he added. "Again."

"If Jimmy hadn't been there we'd both be at the bottom of the bay," Orson said.

"Thank you both for what you did," I said. "Saved Lauren's life."

They nodded and gave me looks that let me know they understood and really received my gratitude.

"I realize you saved everybody," I said, "but I'm most grateful for you saving Lauren."

This time when Ernie nodded there was an even deeper sadness in his eyes.

"I'm gonna do the same for you, pal," I said. "Gonna find Joan and get her back."

He nodded again. "Never doubted it. We're getting close. I can feel it."

"Howell wants to talk to us about what happened," I said. "And they've got to get the coroner over here to get Mary Pat's body. But they're gonna be a while. You guys wanna walk over to Bird of Paradise with us for a drink and a little dinner while we wait?"

"The queer joint?" Ernie asked.

I nodded.

"Where's that?" Orson asked.

"In that shack on the dock out over Masalina Bayou."

"Oh. And it's queer?"

"Jimmy," Ernie said, "I don't think you realize how much you've changed since we knew you."

"Must not," I said. "'Cause it doesn't seem like I have to me."

"Really? Negro partner. Jap secretary. Living with a woman outside of wedlock. Fraternizing with fags."

"Fraternizing with friends."

"Why?"

"I genuinely like Tommy and his place. It's also one of the few places I can go with my Negro partner and Jap secretary and—"

"The woman you're living in sin with," Orca said without looking up from the pile of clothes he was sorting through. He said it to be helpful. There was nothing sarcastic or malicious in his remark.

"And her. My wife out of wedlock."

"Better count us out of this one, partner," Ernie said.

His reasons were ugly and unbecoming but I understood where they came from. I didn't like it, but I didn't have to.

"IT COULD'VE BEEN A LOT WORSE," David Howell was saying.

We were in the empty USO building—me and Lauren, Clip and Miki, Ernie and Orca, and now Howell.

Ernie looked like he was about to go out for a night on the town, but Orca looked to be popping out of kids' clothes—had in fact ripped the seams of the largest coat and pants he could find just to get them on.

"Looks like all we lost was one victory ship, one train car, and two men," he said.

"And one brave, generous, kind girl," Lauren added.

"Yes. Sorry. Didn't mean . . . And what you guys did here . . . Can you imagine if it had gone off inside here with a full house?"

"The place was packed," Lauren said.

"Y'all saved a couple of hundred lives at least," he said. "Most of them servicemen."

"Orson's the real hero," I said.

"Yes he is," Ernie added.

"He certainly is," Lauren said. "Took that bomb away from me as if it were nothing at all."

This last caused him to blush.

"With the two y'all got—"

"Not y'all," I said. "Clip."

"I just meant . . . Sorry. With the two Clip got, the two we got, and the one who died in the train car explosion, I'd say there are between one and four still out there—including Demetri."

"Good," Ernie said. "'Cause we're hoping to find him before anyone else does."

38

L auren and I were in our bed, our naked bodies warm beneath several blankets.

Tommy Dorsey's "In the Blue of Evening" was playing almost desultorily.

Like the night, the room was dark, lit only occasionally by the flickering fingers of distant night lightning.

"I wasn't sure we were ever gonna be like this again," Lauren said. "Really didn't see a way out of that one."

I didn't say anything, just concentrated on not thinking about the alternate outcomes of tonight's predicament.

"Wonder if Ernie and Joan will ever get to do what we're doing right now?" she said.

"He disapproves of . . . well, of me," I said. "Of the way I live, of the places I go and who I associate with."

"Surely you know most everyone does, darling," she said. "Disapprove of you and me not being married. Of your relationship with Clip. Miki. Tommy. Mama Cora. Just for starters."

"Different when it's a close friend," I said. "At least one who used to be close. He's supposed to . . ."

"Accept you?"

"Sure, but not just," I said. "He's supposed to trust me, to reevaluate his conditioned responses because it involves his friend."

She let out a little laugh.

"What? Is that so much to ask?"

"I'm afraid so, sweetheart. But I adore you for thinking it shouldn't be."

"Makes me sad," I said.

"You've lost your friends in a way," she said.

She was right. I had. And it made me more sad than I could say, but the loss was nothing at all compared to what had been gained—genuine friendship with authentic, honorable people and a love the likes of which poetry can't contain or even explain.

IN MY DREAM, Ernie, Orson, and I were playing sandlot baseball after school on a seemingly endless North Florida spring day.

Ernie was pitching. I was on second. Orca was at bat.

Then something dissonant, something wrong, pushed its way into my unconscious.

I woke to the sounds of Lauren whimpering.

The covers were off and I was cold.

"You having a bad dream?" I asked, reaching for her.

She was out from beneath the covers too.

And someone was on top of her.

"Turn on light," the disembodied voice in the darkness said.

The voice belonged to a German male.

I rolled the other way, reached over, and turned on the lamp.

Blinking in the blinding light, it took me a moment to be able to see. When the blurry shapes finally came into focus, I saw something I wish I never had.

Demetri, as naked as we were, on top of Lauren, his pistol pressed into her mouth.

"You will watch while I make fuck on your girl," he said. "Try anything and I blow back of her head off."

Tears were streaming down her cheeks.

I had never felt as vulnerable or as weak or as naked in my life.

"Look at me," I said to her.

Unable to move her head because of the gun, she cut her eyes over toward me.

"I love you. It's going to be okay. Just keep looking at me."

I tried to think of what to say and do. There was no way I was going to lie here and let him rape Lauren beside me, even if it meant we would both die—and not just because he'd kill us anyway when he was done.

His left hand was holding the gun pressed into Lauren's mouth. His right was rubbing his flaccid penis, attempting to coax the uninspired organ into becoming the weapon he wanted it to be.

I thought about what might disarm him the most, what my best chance against him might be.

"Just keep looking at me," I said. "Think of me while he does what he does to you. Okay? Just think of me."

Was that enough to make him think I wasn't going to put up a fight? Was I a weak, one-armed, passive coward?

He continued rubbing his limp genitals, leering at her bare breasts as he did.

"You burn your woman or someone else do it for you?" he said.

Like before he didn't look at me, just continued to stare at the beautiful body of my beloved—the last thing he was ever going to see in this life.

Certain he wasn't looking, I gave Lauren a small nod and a look that said I was about to make my move.

"Just keep looking at me, baby," I said. "Don't buck or thrust, just lie there and take it. It's going to be okay. He's got a little dick and he's not going to be able to get it up anyway."

That got his attention.

In the split second he turned his attention toward me, starting to pull the gun out of Lauren's mouth presumably to shoot me, she bucked up and I rolled. Rolling into him and on top of her, the momentum carried us both off Lauren and crashing to the floor, the gun firing as we did.

Lauren remained on the bed behind us and I couldn't see if she had been shot or not.

Had I gotten her killed? Was all this for nothing? Was everything?

He still had possession of the pistol.

With my one hand, I grabbed for it.

We were two naked men wrestling for a gun on the floor, but I couldn't afford to feel awkward or inhibited in any way.

I had hold of the gun, but so did he, and I couldn't do anything with it, couldn't gain any advantage.

Then he brought his right hand up and grabbed with it too.

My one arm was no match for his two.

He began turning the pistol toward me, lifting it as he did.

I tried with all my might, but it was no good.

He was lifting the gun to shoot me in the face and I couldn't stop it.

God damn I hated being so fuckin' weak and useless.

I was going to die and then what was he going to do to Lauren —whether she was still alive or dead herself?

I couldn't bear the thought of that.

Pulling my leg back, I kneed him in the nuts as hard as I could.

He let out a wicked yelp but didn't stop bringing the pistol up toward my face.

Think. Try something else. Anything. Come on.

It was no good. I couldn't think of anything else to do.

His finger was on the trigger now and the gun was nearly pointed at me.

He squeezed off a round that just barely missed my neck. It shattered one of Lauren's perfume bottles and ricocheted off the record player.

The pistol kept turning despite my best efforts.

The next round would rattle around my brainpan and unspringing my mortal coil.

"I love you Lauren," I said, not sure if she was conscious to hear me.

Out of the corner of my eye, I saw the blue-black barrel of my revolver coming past me and down toward Demetri.

Lauren was there, leaning against me, reaching down with the weapon.

When she had the barrel in position, she pulled the trigger and shot Demetri in the face. Twice.

"I love you too," she said.

39

Samuel Wineberger and his wife Vivian lived in a plush, palatial home on the bay in the Cove.

Before they grew old, retired, and returned to this place where he had grown up, they had been one of Hollywood's most celebrated couples toward the end of the silent film era. Transitioning from stage to screen, he directed and she starred in hit after hit, but they had been unable to successfully make the transition into talking pictures.

We were seated in their glassed-in Florida room overlooking their backyard and its fifty-yard drop-off into the bay.

It was a sunny, clear morning, and the bay was brilliant in its brightness and beauty, calm and expansive. Though it was cold out, you couldn't tell it from in this hothouse-like room.

I was sleepy, having spent much of the night dealing with Demetri, and the sun and warmth weren't helping. Following the cops and the cleanup, Lauren and I had checked into our old room at the Cove Hotel, where she was fast asleep right now.

Sam, in silk pajamas and robe, was in a high-back wooden wheelchair with a wicker back, a blue blanket across his lap.

Vivian floated around the room in a flowing white gown

making us tea and seeing to her husband's needs. Her hair and makeup were immaculate, her every move a performance.

Ray and I had found their niece and some of Vivian's jewelry she had taken a few years back and I had stayed in touch with them ever since.

"Such a shame about Ray," Sam said.

"Such an awful shame," Vivian echoed as she served me my tea in fine china.

As if she had become what she had pretended to be for so long, all of Vivian's expressions were greatly exaggerated— conveying enough emotion for the last row of the theater to see what her character was supposed to be feeling.

"Now there was an interesting man who cut a classic figure," Sam said. "I could've cast him in a crime picture and made it a hit and him a star."

I nodded.

Having finished serving the tea, Vivian had floated over to the chair next to Sam's wheelchair and glided into it, leaning forward and crossing her legs in the most dramatic way possible, and had her hand beneath her chin as she gazed with intensity at whoever was talking, her head bobbing back and forth between the two of us as if she were watching the slowest, but most interesting tennis match in history.

"Lots of crime pictures bein' made these days," he said. "Cheap B pictures, but they got somethin'. Style. They got style for days."

"It's pictures that bring me by to see you today," I said.

"Oh yeah? Why's that?"

"Missing girl I'm looking for told a friend she had been discovered by a location scout and a casting director who were here in town working on a new picture. You know anything about that?"

"Here?"

"Here?" Vivian said. "In Panama City?"

She had a deep, throaty smoker's voice with a good bit of Southern twang, as if your manly old aunt maid had burned her vocal chords with lots of hard booze and too many cigarettes. Like the guys said to have a face for radio, she definitely had a voice for silent pictures.

"That's what she said."

"Could be," Sam said. "Two likely scenarios. Lots of war pictures being made. Not full movies. Training. Propaganda. News reels. Could be something like that."

I nodded.

"The other thing it could be . . . Since the war, a lot of European directors have come over and started working here. Some of them very experimental—with varying degrees of success—"

"Very varying degrees of success," Vivian said.

"Some of them film on location as much as possible," he said. "Avoid the studio sound stages any chance they get. Jean Renoir shot *Swamp Water* just a few hours from here in Georgia a couple of years back."

"With Walter Brennan and Dana Andrews," Vivian said. "I just adore Dana. Adore him."

"That's the picture she told her friend they had worked on," I said.

"Then it's probably legit," he said. "Unless they knew enough to lie to her. It's easy enough to find out. Bring me the phone, Viv."

Made in 1941, *Swamp Water* was director Jean Renoir's first American film. Starring Walter Brennan and Walter Huston, Anne Baxter, and Dana Andrews, it was produced at 20th Century Fox. Shot on location in the Okefenokee Swamp near Waycross, Georgia, the film, based on the Vereen Bell novel, is about a local boy, Ben (Dana Andrews), who encounters a fugitive Tom Keefer (Walter Brennan) from a murder charge while hunting in the Okefenokee Swamp. The two form a partnership in which Ben sells the animals hunted and trapped by both until townsfolk become suspicious.

When Sam hung up the phone, the expression beneath his raised eyebrows was one of surprised amusement.

"It's legit," he said. "They're keeping it quiet, which is why I didn't know about it yet, but they want to do a war picture here, using Tyndall Field, the naval section base, Wainwright Shipyard, and Camp Gordon Johnston near Carrabelle. I've set up a meeting for you with them this afternoon."

40

When I got back to the office I found Miki distraught. She ran to me the moment I reached the top of the stairs.

"They take Clip," she said between sobs.

"Who?"

"Cop. Say he rape white woman last night. Say he gonna get what comin' to him."

"Which cop?" I said. "Did he give his name?"

"Clip say tell Jimmy that Dixon have him."

Freddie Dixon was a cop who rightly or wrongly believed Clip had had an affair with his wife a while back and had it in for him. At one point when I was still part of PCPD, Dixon along with his crooked cop buddy Gerald Whitfield thought they finally had Clip for stolen merchandise, which was just an excuse to get their hands on him. Their plan had been to get him into custody where some very bad things would befall him—after which he'd get shot trying to escape. I had stopped them and Clip and I had become fast friends.

"Shit. How long ago was it?"

"Half the hour so."

"Call Folsom. Tell him what's going on. If you can't get him, try Howell. Let them know I'm on my way over there. I doubt Dixon took him to the station, but that's where I'll start."

She didn't move.

"Miki, look at me. It's going to be okay. I'll get him back. I need you to simmer down and make the calls, okay?"

She nodded.

"Take a deep breath and let it out slowly. Calm down and concentrate on what we need to do to get him back. I need your help to do it."

"Miki better," she said. "You go. Everything okay Jakey."

"Call Lauren after you talk to Folsom. She's at the Cove Hotel. Let her know what's going on. Ask her to help you calm down. When Ernie and Orson get here, fill them in and tell them to wait here for me."

To my surprise, Freddie Dixon had actually brought Clip to police headquarters and booked him.

"It ain't personal," he was saying. "Not anymore."

The four of us were in Folsom's office—Howell, Dixon, Folsom, and me.

"I got him this time fair and square. I knew I would eventually. It was just a matter of givin' him enough rope and lettin' him do the rest. This is legit. I ain't playin' no angles or nothin'. Strictly by the book."

"When was this alleged to have happened?" I asked.

Dixon looked at Folsom. "Do I have to answer the questions of some low-rent, one-armed peeper?"

"When did she say it happened?" Folsom asked. "Unless you mind answering my questions too?"

"Last night," he said.

"What time?" I asked.

He ignored me.

"What time?" Folsom asked.

"No matter what time I say, he's gonna say the nigger was with him at that time," he said.

"Actually," Howell said, "Clip was with me part of the night. And helping to disarm a bomb at the USO the other part. We were dealing with some major attempted sabotage last night, or didn't you hear?"

"Yeah, I heard. I was out there helping like all the rest."

"What time?"

"Around eleven."

"He was with me and a handful of other people, at least two of them war heroes, at the USO at that time," Howell said.

"Then maybe she got the time mixed up," he said. "She's a credible witness. No reason to lie. She's from a good family. Got a good job at the phone company. Why would she—"

"Her name wouldn't happen to be Betty Blackmon, would it?" I said.

"Yeah, why?"

"No nigger's gonna put his dirty hands on me," Betty Blackmon was saying to Folsom. "He needs to be strung up. What kind of town has this become?"

Folsom, Howell, and Dixon were in an interview room with Betty Blackmon. I was observing from behind the two-way glass.

"What time did the attack happen?" Folsom asked.

"A little after eleven last night."

"Where?"

"He broke into my home and . . ."

Her lip started to quiver and she began to cry.

"It was so awful."

"How do you know it was Mr. Jones?"

"*Mister*? That's rich. You're callin' a nigger rapist *mister*? Because of his eye. His missing eye. I had to look at that horrible thing while he ..."

"Miss Blackmon," Folsom said. "This is one of my top men, Detective Howell."

"How do you do?" she said.

"Mr. Jones was with him during the time you say the attack happened last night."

"Then I was wrong about the time," she said. "Or the night. Maybe it was the night before."

"Was it?" Dixon said. "Could it have been the night before?"

"Yeah. That's it. It was the night before."

"Miss Blackmon," Folsom said. "Let me tell you something. What you're doing is far more dangerous than you realize. In another department, another accused, you could have very easily gotten an innocent man killed—maybe even without a trial. That's murder."

"He's a nigger," she said.

"If you ever try anything like this again, I'll arrest you. Do you understand?"

"Then get ready to arrest me," she said. "That nigger took everything from me. Everything. And I will get him back."

"Arrest," Folsom said.

"Gladly," Howell said.

"For what?"

"Perverting the course of justice," he said. "Lying to a police officer. Attempted murder. Wasting my time. And generally being a sick little sister."

Most of it wasn't real. None of it would stick. But she'd spend a night or two in jail and be given an opportunity to reflect and reconsider and actually alter the course of her life—an opportunity she would no doubt not take.

41

When I thought about what could have so easily happened to Clip, I experienced equal parts anger and anxiety.

Life could be so precarious and capricious—for some far more than others.

For most of the drive back to the office, Clip had been quiet.

"You okay?" I asked.

He nodded.

"What is it?" I said.

He shrugged. "Just thinkin'."

"I'm trying not to think of what could've happened," I said. "Of what a woman like that could've done. She could've so easily gotten you killed."

"I'd be dead already if it weren't for you," he said.

"The reverse of that is also true," I said. "But . . . I just can't believe we live in a world where it takes so little to . . ."

"What? String up a nigger? Usually take far less than that. And most Negroes don't have a Jimmy Riley to rush down to headquarters—or could do anything if they did."

"A woman like that does so much damage," I said.

"Need to be put down," he said. "Her and Dixon both. He not gonna stop 'til he make me do it. Not sure about her."

I thought about what she had said, about her getting Clip back for the perceived injury she believed he had inflicted.

He let out a harsh, humorless laugh. "Felt so good solving that case, exposing that bitch and her twisted little scheme. So fuckin' full of myself. Negro Holmes. Shee-it."

He shook his head and went somewhere I couldn't go.

"World not ready for no Negro private eye," he said. "Thanks for the opportunity just the same. You never gonna know what it meant to me that you . . . did what you did."

I tried to talk him out of it, but it was no good.

"Please just take a little time to think about it, okay?" I said.

He shook his head.

"I need you," I said. "Really can't do any of this without you."

He shook his head. "Just can't. Not anymore."

"But—"

"Know how to survive in my world," he said. "Not in this one. Too exposed, too . . . Not gonna make myself such a big target. Not for motherfuckers like them."

When we pulled up and parked, he said, "Tell Miki I'a be by for her after work."

INSIDE THE OFFICE, I found Ernie and Orca waiting for me.

"Hiya, Jimmy," Orson said. "How's tricks?"

"I need to talk to you," Ernie said.

"Okay," I said. "Give me just a minute. Y'all wait in my office, will you?"

They agreed to and went in, leaving Miki and me alone in the reception area.

"Where is Clip?" she asked. "What going on?"

"He's okay," I said. "We straightened everything out. He's not in jail any—"

She dropped the files she was holding onto her desk and hugged me hard and long.

"Thank you so much, Jimmy-san. You real hero to Miki Matsumoto. Again."

She held on for a few moments more, then after one more tight squeeze, released me.

"Where Clip now?"

"It really got to him," I said.

She nodded. "He okay you say."

"Something about the way this went down after the way you guys solved the case . . . He just . . . He says he's done. Not coming back. I'm hoping he'll change his mind. You can talk to him about it this evening. He said he'd be by to pick you up after work."

Everything about her countenance dropped, her face a heartrending mask of sadness and confusion.

"I'm sorry," I said.

"I've got the best lead so far," I said. "I found the location scout and casting director Joan may have met. We're meeting with them this afternoon."

"That's great," Ernie said, but there was something in the way he said it that let me know he really didn't believe it was.

"What's wrong?" I asked.

"Huh? Nothin'. It's good news."

"So why don't you sound like it is?"

He shrugged.

"What did you want to talk to me about?" I asked.

He cut his eyes over at Orca.

"Hey big fella, would you mind checkin' on Miki. She's upset about something that happened this morning. Mind talkin' to her a few minutes?"

"No, I don't mind," he said, pushing his enormous frame up from the chair I was sure was going to break. "But if you guys wanna talk without me, just say so. You ain't gotta make up shit for me to do."

"She really is upset and needs comforting," I said.

"She told us what happened to Clip," Ernie said.

"He's out, but says he's not coming back to work here."

Orca lumbered out of the room and closed the door.

The moment he did, Ernie said, "Orson's grandmother confided in me," he said. "She lied. He wasn't with her when the second woman was killed. He doesn't have an alibi for either murder, Jimmy. I think he killed those prostitutes. I've seen enough just watching him over the past few days . . . He's far worse than I realized."

"You really think he could've—"

"I do. And I'll tell you something else. The girl at the USO—what was her name? Linda Sue. He had already met with her. She had already told him about the movie guys and Joan bein' discovered by them. What if . . . What if he already found her and killed her too? It would explain why he's blocking out so much, why he can't remember, why he supposedly couldn't find her, and why we can't now. He killed her and buried the body."

"God, I hope not," I said. "But either way. Let's go find out."

42

E rnie was on edge.

I was filled with a deep sense of dread.

Orca seemed oblivious to both.

"The Three Musketeers riding together again," he said from the backseat. "This is going to be a blast, ain't it fellas?"

We were heading toward Wewahitchka on Highway 22, the afternoon sun behind us slanting in the back window, reflecting off all the mirrors and shiny surfaces.

Working mostly between Carrabelle and Panama City Beach, Sid Bowen and Len Hammond, the two men working on the pre-production of *Victory is Ours* had set up their headquarters in a rented fish camp on the Apalachicola River.

I was driving, Ernie fidgeting in the passenger seat beside me, dark energy emanating off him like heat shimmering off an asphalt highway at midday.

He had missed a small patch on his left cheek while shaving and he absently but continually worried at the whiskers with a thumbnail.

Suddenly, Ernie spun around in the seat and engaged Orson. "Remembered anything else yet?" he asked.

"About what?"

"*About what*? Are you kidding? Can you believe this guy? About what. The two girls that got killed. Anybody else you talked to about Joan. Anything at all."

"No, Ernie, not so far."

"Are you trying?" he said. "I don't think you're trying."

"I am."

"And you can't come up with anything?"

"Not so far."

"Are you blocking something bad out?" Ernie said. "Is that it?"

"I don't know. I . . . I'm . . . just not sure."

Ernie shook his head.

The rural highway was empty and straight and shimmering, the woods on either side thick, vibrant, and sun-kissed.

"Easy," I said.

"Are you mad at me, Ernie?" Orca asked.

"You don't remember Linda Sue telling you all the stuff about Joan before?"

"I don't. I mean . . . I kinda do now. But I didn't. Is that why you're mad?"

"Did you find out where Joan went?" Ernie said.

"I don't know. I just . . ."

He began to hit his head with his fists.

"Hey," I said. "Orson. Look at me. Stop that. It's okay. Ernie's just anxious to find Joan. You understand."

Ernie turned back around in the seat and Orca seem to settle down a little.

I would've had a bad feeling no matter where we were headed, but returning to the place where Ray and I had shot each other only added to the visceral sense of foreboding I felt.

As we neared the small town, I couldn't shake the feeling that we were driving toward a fate far worse than any of us could imagine.

Was Joan dead? Was that it? Or was it worse? Did her disappearance involve betrayal? Torture like Miki's had?

When we turned onto the twisting, turning, treacherous Lake Grove Road, the road that wound its way to dead end into the Apalachicola River at the landing simply known as the End of the Road, I relived the fateful night I had come here to confront Ray Parker. It had only been a few short months, but seemed like a couple of lifetimes ago, and I was filled with an even deeper, more profound sense of dread.

My pulse quickened as we turned off the paved street onto the dirt road that would lead us to our meeting. But what exactly were we meeting with?

We had to pass Ray's old fish camp on the Dead Lakes to get to the one Sid and Len were renting. There was no other way. If there had been I would've taken it—even if it meant driving a hundred miles out of the way.

As we passed his place, I tried not to look. I really did, but something drew my eyes to it, a force beyond my control.

There in the yard, Ray was standing up, dusting himself off, placing his hat on his head and his gun in its holster, seeming oblivious to the bleeding bullet hole in his heart.

Had I died there too that night? Is that why I kept seeing him? Were the scars on my body actually open wounds—wounds I refused to see for what they were?

As we passed by, Ray tipped his hat toward me and nodded, his knowing expression one of warmth and welcome.

He said something.

Had I just imagined it was *All hope abandon ye who enter here*?

The whole thing is in your imagination, a voice inside me said.

Is it? another asked.

Through me you pass into the city of woe:

Through me you pass into eternal pain:

Through me among the people lost for aye.

Justice the founder of my fabric mov'd:

To rear me was the task of power divine,
Supremest wisdom, and primeval love.
Before me things create were none, save things
Eternal, and eternal I endure.
All hope abandon ye who enter here.

The day dimmed as the sun ducked behind a bank of clouds, a gray haze invading the cypress trees that were now casting soft craggy shadows on the floor of the swamp.

Haunted.

This mysterious place was haunted for me—and always would be.

43

S id Bowen and Len Hammond were so hospitable, so likable, so seemingly genuinely innocuous, that I soon abandoned most of my dread, allowing it to dissipate and drift downstream, winding its way with the river toward the Apalachicola Bay.

They welcomed us into their rented, rustic cabin built in cypress trees up over the river at the end of a long wooden walkway, as if we had been invited guests.

Not only were they gentle and peaceful people, but they were older men, artists, not the sort you'd expect to do harm to a young girl. They seemed anxious to help us find out what happened to Joan.

Sid nodded the moment Ernie showed him the photograph. "That's her," he said. "She was here about . . . what . . . a week and a half ago."

"Just like we told him," Len said, nodding toward Orson.

"*Him*?" Ernie said.

They both nodded and the dread crept back into me. Heavier this time. And darker.

"I was here?" Orson asked.

"You don't remember?" Sid said.

"You did seem quite agitated," Len added. "You were in the war, right?"

"Our picture is partially about that," Sid said.

"About what?" Ernie said.

"The thousand yard stare," he said. "Shell shock. The impact of combat."

"When was this?" Ernie said. "When was he here?"

"Had to be . . . You know I'm not sure. Not long after she was."

"Oh really."

"Let's get back to Joan," I said. "Tell us about—"

"We saw her in Panama City and thought she was perfect for a part in the picture," Len said. "We just mentioned it to her and she was off to the races. It's way early in the process, but she insisted on meeting with us, wanted to talk about every aspect of the project, wanted to meet the director."

"We never expected her to show up out here, but she did," Sid said.

"Really surprised us."

"Asked if we could film her and show the footage to the director," Sid said.

"Did you?" I asked.

"We did. There was no telling that girl *no*, nosiree."

"Can we see the footage?" I said.

"Sure," Len said. "Take me a minute to set up the projector, but if you're willing to wait."

"We'll wait," Ernie said.

While Len set it all up, Sid continued to talk. "She was such a sweet girl. Said it had been a lifelong dream of hers to act. Said this opportunity was destiny and she wasn't about to let it pass her by. Said her fiancé was going to be so surprised and proud of her."

Ernie's lip quivered and he blinked back tears.

Even on the makeshift screen and small, poor, projection

system, Joan looked like she belonged in pictures. The camera loved her, and either imbued her with an—or more likely captured her on—inmate elegance and luminosity.

"She's so beautiful," Orson said, his voice filled with an airy wonder and a childlike innocence.

The test shots were simple. Just Joan walking toward, then away from, then back toward the camera. Turning. Spinning. Posing.

No makeup. No lights. No sound. Just Joan.

"Did you develop this here or send it off?" I asked.

"Here."

"Did you send it to the director?"

He shook his head. "Not yet. Like I said it's a bit premature. I do plan on showing it to him though. Or I did."

"You remembering anything?" Ernie said to Orson.

Orson looked around the room, rubbing his head, a frightened expression on his face. He shook his head. "Sorry, Ernie. I really am."

"She was so happy when she left here," Sid said. "I remember because it was raining and overcast and her mood was so sunny. So hopeful. Such good energy. I hope she's okay and that you find her soon."

44

"So we know she came here," I said.

"And Orca did too," Ernie said.

We were back in the car, driving around the curves of the twisting and turning Lake Grove Road.

"This is the biggest lead we've had since we started looking," I said.

"No," Ernie said. "One of us has had it the whole time."

He had his eyepatch off and the still-seeping wound was blood-red and angry, matching his mood. The white tip of the bandage on his hand was turning crimson too.

Orca was silent in the backseat. He wasn't saying anything, but he was reacting to every veiled accusation being made by Ernie. Sweat popping out on his face and forehead. Heavy sighs. Deepening scowl. Narrowing, angry eyes. Pursing lips. Clenching fists. Veins bulging out of his neck.

Trying to figure out our next move and to get Ernie to ease up on Orca, I said, "If Sid and Len didn't have anything to do with her disappearance, and I really don't think they did, then we have to find out where she went after she left the camp."

Neither of them said anything.

"We should ask around town," I said.

"Or we could just ask Orca," Ernie said.

He turned in the seat to face the seething behemoth. "Where is she?" he said. "What'd you do to her?"

"Ernie—"

"Did you catch up to her and think she was cheating on me? Did you lose it? Have one of your blackouts and beat her to death like you did the two prostitutes?"

"Stop it."

"What're you doin'?" I said.

"Your grandmother told me she lied to the police," Ernie said. "Said you weren't with her, that you really don't have an alibi after all. You killed them."

"No. Stop. Stop saying those things."

"Notice how no more hookers have been killed since we've been watching you?" Ernie said.

"No, that's not—"

"That plate in your head has infected your brain, pal. You're a stone cold killer. You're a killer of women, a—"

"NO. TAKE IT BACK. NOW."

"Or what? You'll beat on me? Well, let me tell you somethin', pal. I ain't no woman. Just try something. Try that shit on a man."

Orson was losing it and it was obvious Ernie wanted him to.

"Finding Joan is what we should be working on," I said.

"Whatta you think I'm doing?" Ernie said. "Where'd you put her body? Where is my girl? Where'd you do it, you big, dumb bastard."

Reaching back over the seat, Ernie began slapping Orson in the face.

With only one arm, I couldn't do anything to stop him and keep a hand on the wheel. I decided to find a place to pull off the road and try to get things back under—

But I was too late.

When Orca struck, it was fierce and furious and ferocious.

He pounced with far more speed and agility than I would have thought he was capable of.

Grabbing Ernie's head with both his big mitts, he began to squeeze and pull, as if he were simultaneously trying to crush Ernie's skull and rip his head off.

Flailing desperately, realizing he only had moments to live, Ernie did the worst thing he could do. He reached over, grabbed the wheel, which was completely exposed on the side closest to him because of my missing right, and pulled.

He was trying to do anything to pull himself free of the bear trap his head was stuck in. He was desperate. Not thinking. Only reacting.

He jerked the wheel out of my hand and the car off the road.

Flipping end over end, we careened into a guardrail, then over it, down into the swamp, end over end another time or two before coming to rest upside down against a stand of ancient hardwoods.

45

Ernie's lifeless eyes looked up at me from the unnaturally wrenched neck of his body crumpled like laundry on the passenger-side floorboard. It was strange. They were Ernie's eyes but they weren't. They had no light in them, no presence behind them, and they looked as eerie as those of a lifelike doll's.

The car was at a steep angle in a swamp hole, its nose pointing down, its back end up in the air a few feet off the ground.

I looked in the backseat. It was empty. In fact, it was missing. It appeared as though Orca had ripped it out and crawled out through the trunk.

I decided to go out that same way when I realized my door was wedged against an oak tree.

Slowly, carefully, crawling over the front seat, across the bottom seat of the back, and up out of the trunk.

The forest floor of the hardwood hammock was damp dirt, slick leaves, and pine straw, and I had a hard time getting any traction.

I found Orca passed out, facedown on the ground about

twenty yards from the car.

"Hey," I said, shaking him. "Orson."

"Jimmy? Where are we? What—"

"Come on, big fella, let's get out of here. We had a wreck and we need to go get help. We're gonna have to walk along the road until we come to a house or a vehicle comes by."

"Where's Ahab?"

"He'll have to wait here for us," I said. "Come on, let's go get help. Can you walk?"

~

WE CLIMBED up to the road using part of the bent guardrail.

I looked both ways and saw nothing coming.

Back toward the landing to Sid and Len's or in the opposite direction toward town?

I thought I remembered a small cabin in the direction of town not from here. Of course, we could come to Ray's first, but I wasn't stopping there.

We headed in the direction of the other cabin and beyond it town.

On either side of the road, the dense river swamp grew with such verdant variety it seemed prehistoric.

The late afternoon sun was low in the sky, the lengthening shadows of pine, cypress, and oak trees growing all around us.

Ernie is dead. Is that really possible?

We walked a mile or more in silence along the winding road without seeing anyone.

Orson didn't seem out of sorts in any way, just out with his old friend on an evening constitutional.

As the day grew dimmer, the noises from the river swamp grew louder.

When we reached the last and most severe curve before Ray's old fish camp, I could see a small glint of metal some fifty yards or more out in the woods. There didn't appear to be an opening in the seemingly impenetrable tree line, but the trajectory was such that it could easily be that of a car that missed the curve and careened straight out into the swamp.

"Look at that," I said.

"What? I don't— Is it a car?"

"Could be."

"Want me to take a closer look?" he said. "You could stay here and flag down help if somebody comes by."

"Just go a little closer to see what it is."

"Sure thing, Jimmy."

If it was a vehicle, it had left no sign in the edge of the swamp that it had entered here. There wasn't even an opening big enough for Orca to pass through.

He fought his way through and after twenty yards or so yelled back, "It's a car. And Jimmy, it looks like it could be Joan's."

"Wait for me," I said. "I want to—"

"I better come back and help you," he said. "It's rough going."

He came back and helped, and in fifteen minutes or so we were approaching the car that matched the description of Joan's.

"You think Sid and Len did something with her and hid her car in here?" Orson asked.

I shook my head.

"I think the road was wet, it was hard to see in the rain, and she missed the curve, just kept driving straight when the road turned," I said. "We'll know in a minute."

The car was caked with dust and dirt and tree branches, but I could make out a figure inside.

I tried the handle but was unable to open it.

"Here," Orson said. "Let me try."

He tried it, but it wouldn't give. Then he jerked on it so hard I thought he was going to rip the entire door off. It gave then and swung open to reveal the decaying body of Joan Wynn inside.

The victim of a truly tragic accident, a tragic accident that led to more tragedy.

"I didn't kill her," Orca said in an exclamation that could only be described as childlike.

"No, you didn't," I said. "A rainy road and the swamp did."

"I didn't kill those other girls either," he said. "I'm sure of it now. Ernie's gonna be so happy when he—"

I could see the terrible truth come into his eyes. "Ernie . . ." he said. "I . . . oh God, I . . . I . . ."

He couldn't bring himself to say it and I couldn't blame him.

Life is random and capricious, I thought. *Death merciless and meaningless.*

We had done what we had set out to do. We had found Joan and reunited her with her Ernie. Their lifeless bodies were lying less than two miles apart inside vehicles in an unforgiving river swamp that would quickly consume them if we didn't reclaim them soon. The would-be movie star and the war hero who loved, her tragically dying in an eerie mire haunted by Ray Parker. And who knows, maybe Lauren and I are still here too.

46

Orson had only two requests.

I intended to honor them both.

He wanted to turn himself in and he wanted to do it to the reserved, gentle David Howell.

There was nothing I could do for Ernie or Joan now, so I was going to do all I could for one of the few friends I had left.

We climbed back up to the road and continued toward town.

Eventually, a truck came by and gave us a ride to a phone at the general store in town.

The general store was a two-story tin building, with offices and living quarters for the Listers, who owned and operated it, upstairs.

I called Lauren first.

"Where are you?" she asked. "Have you spoken to Miki or David Howell?"

"No. Why?"

"Another woman was murdered last night and they got the guy who did it. He confessed to the other two also. Orson's innocent."

I turned and looked at my big, bumbling friend, who was

seated in the corner staring off at something no one but him would ever be able to see.

"Did you hear me? Are you there?"

"Who was it?"

"Guy named Charles Simmons. Howell said you referred to him as Sweaty Neck. Says Orson embarrassed him and he targeted the other two girls to try to frame him."

I thought about it. Had I been able to feel anything at all, I'd want to cry.

"Jimmy? What is it? What's wrong?"

I told her.

"Oh my God, Jimmy, I'm so sorry. Are you okay?"

"There's a guy here who's going to give us a ride back over," I said. "We'll let Orca turn himself in, tell Howell everything and let him coordinate with the cops here to recover the bodies and process the crime scenes."

"Just get back to me as soon as you can," she said. "I keep trying to sleep, but nightmares get the better of me. Need you beside me."

"I will be as soon as I can," I said. "Demetri is no longer a threat—thanks to you. He can't hurt you or anyone else."

"I keep thinking about what I did," she said. "How I . . . shot him in the . . ."

"You did what you had to to save my life—and yours. Think about what he would have done to you after he shot me. Killing someone is . . . There's nothing quite like it in the world—even when he was a monster and left you no choice. We'll get through it together. I'll be there for you. Thanks to you, I'll be there. We'll be together."

"Miki told me about Clip. You've been through so much. Come let me take care of you."

"I'll be there," I said. "Soon as I can."

Next I called Howell, but I got Folsom.

"He's not here right now," he said. "He's checkin' out a tip we got on a possible hideout of the other saboteurs. It came from your friend. What's her name?"

"Mama Cora?"

"Yeah. Called David when she couldn't find you."

"Will you tell him I need to see him tonight, to wait for me at headquarters or come to my office. I'm in Wewa and will be back in town in about an hour."

"Anything I can do?"

"Yeah," I said. "Make sure he gets the message."

47

W hen we finally found David Howell it wasn't at my office or police headquarters, but in an airplane hangar at Tyndall Field.

He and another officer I didn't recognize were standing on an anti-tank land mine surrounded by enough explosives to blow up a city block.

Orson and I had arrived at the police station to find Henry Folsom leaving. He had explained the situation to us and we had asked to accompany him.

"Not much we can do but tell him goodbye," he said. "And we may all get killed trying to do that, but you're welcome to join me."

The final part of the Nazi's plot was to blow up as many aircraft at Tyndall Field as possible.

Entering by boat through the bay and pulling wagons piled with explosives through the woods, the three remaining sabo-teurs had been sneaking into a seldom-used hangar at night and stockpiling their weapons.

Though the hangar was rarely used, it was close to several

that were and routinely had planes all around it—particularly at night.

Tonight, Howell and two other officers had followed the Nazis across the bay, through the woods, and into the hangar.

Two of the three saboteurs had been shot and killed, but not before Howell and one of the other officers had stepped onto and engaged an anti-tank mine positioned to detonate the entire hangar full of explosives and the many planes surrounding it.

Not wanting to be killed in the explosion, the surviving saboteur had drawn the two men's attention to where they were standing and warned them not to move, before fleeing only to be captured a little later.

The other officer had called Folsom who had in turn talked to Tyndall Field, who had been evacuating aircraft ever since.

Orson and I had entered the hangar with Folsom to find Howell and the other officer standing on the pressure plate of a large anti-tank land mine.

"It was an anti-personnel one of these that cost me my right foot," Howell said. "Never told y'all that, did I?"

"No," I said. "You never did."

"Can't believe I survive the nightmare I did over there to come home to still get killed by the goddamn Nazis."

No one said anything.

Unlike the anti-personnel land mines that detonated as soon as they were stepped on, some of the anti-tank devices, like the one they were standing on, were triggered when driven over or in this case stepped on, but wouldn't explode until the weight was lifted. The delay allowed for the explosion to occur under the center of the tank where the armor wasn't as thick as it was in the front in order to do the most damage.

"They moved the planes to a safe distance yet?" Howell asked.

"Most of them," Folsom said. He then moved to the other side to talk to the other officer.

"I guess you guys heard we got the guy who killed the prostitutes?" he said. "No hard feelings I hope. Just doing my job. Had to investigate it all the way. Had to be sure."

"You're a standup guy," Orson said. "So am I. That's why I'm here."

"Whatta you mean?"

Orson told him—with me filling in details here and there.

"Sounds to me like the Nazi's got your friend too," he said. "Got you both."

"They did," he said, "but they ain't gonna get you."

He then put a foot on the pressure plate with them.

Folsom said, "What the hell're you—"

"I weigh about what you guys weigh together," he said. "Step off on three as I put my other foot down."

"One."

"Wait," Howell said. "You don't need to—"

"Two."

"But what if it—"

"Three."

The two men carefully stepped off as Orson brought his other foot down.

"Now get the hell outta here," he said. "Give me a minute alone to prepare to meet my maker."

"Everyone out," Folsom yelled. "Now."

The air force personnel at the edges began to file out of the building.

Everyone around us began to move but me and Howell.

"I don't know what to say," he said.

"Nothing to say," Orson said. "Enjoy your life. Keep up the good work." He then saluted him.

Howell saluted back and walked away.

"You're a true hero, Orson," I said. "You've proved it time and again."

"I'm a coward," he said. "Can't live with what I did."

A line from *The Keys of the Kingdom* that Ernie had underlined came to mind. *Some temptations cannot be fought. One must close one's mind and fly from them.*

"That wasn't you," I said. "Don't take that with you. An explosive device was planted inside you during the war. That's all. It just went off today. The truth is Ernie set it off. Intentionally."

"You're a good friend Jimmy."

"Ernie and Joan are together already," I said. "Tell them hello for me. They're happy. You'll see. Ernie won't blame you for what happened."

"Soon find out," he said. "You'll be joining us too if you don't get of out here. Time to clear out, pal."

"Goodbye, my good friend," I said.

"Goodbye, soldier," he said, and though I had never served, he saluted me too.

———

The blast was enormous.

As befitting a heroic behemoth like Orca.

A thunderous boom, concussive and jarring—even at the one-mile marker designated as the minimum safe distance.

A rolling, roiling ball of black and gray smoke, red and orange fire blasting up into the darkness, temporarily turning the night sky to day.

"He died a hero," Howell said.

"He lived one too," I said.

He nodded. "Yes he did. I owe my life to him."

"A lot of people can say that."

"But," he said, "not a lot of people can have that said about them."

I WAS SO TIRED, so sad, so unbelievably drained, but there was one final thing I had to do before I would be able to join Lauren in our room at the Cove.

Leaving Tyndall Field, I drove straight down 11th Street to Clip's little wooden house.

Miki answered the door.

"Jimmy boss-san. What doing here?"

"He here?" I asked.

She nodded. "Come in."

"Could you get him for me?" I said. "I'll wait out here."

Eventually, Clip joined me on the leaning front porch.

We stood in silence for a while. Eventually I told him what all had happened.

"I've lost Ray, Pete, Ruth Ann, Ernie, Orca," I said. "None of them were a fraction of the friend you are. I can't lose you too."

He didn't say anything.

"And I don't just mean as a friend," I said. "I mean . . . I don't want to do this work without you. You're the reason I started doing it again in the first place."

"Fuckin' Freddy," he said.

Freddy Freeman was Clip's cousin, a boxer we had worked for and Clip had actually fought for.

"We've all been through so much," I said. "Miki more than the rest of us. Been through a war of our own right here at home, but we can figure it all out. I really think we can. We can be more careful and—"

"I's already plannin' on being at work in the mornin'," he said.

"You were?"

He nodded.

"Was."

"Have I talked you out of it?"

"Almost," he said. "Best stop now before you do."

"See you tomorrow?" I said.

And it reminded me of my and Lauren's pledge of *tomorrow and tomorrow and tomorrow.*

He nodded. "See you then," he said, adding after a beat, "partner."

IT WAS LATE when I crawled into bed beside Lauren in our old room at the Cove Hotel.

I was exhausted but not sleepy.

She turned toward me and we held each other in the way only lovers can.

"I'm so glad you're back," she said.

"Sorry it wasn't sooner."

"Are you okay?"

I thought about it before answering her. "Actually," I said. "I am. Right now, in this moment, here with you, I am."

"Good," she said, gently touching my face. "You can mourn your losses later."

She was right. I could and I would.

I would mourn my childhood buddies who wouldn't grow any older than they were on this day. I would mourn the great loss, not just to me, but the world. I would mourn all they didn't get to do, all we didn't get to share, but I'd also remember and be grateful for all we did.

And I wouldn't just mourn the loss of my old friends, but comfort and console and protect my new ones, beginning with Clip and continuing with Miki. And of course Lauren. Always Lauren. We were family and needed to be together.

"Right now," Lauren said, "there isn't loss. There is only what has been found, there is only our love."

What's been lost is as nothing compared to what's been found.

And there was. Only our love. Our life. She was right.

As it so often did, the Emerson quote came to mind.

Finish each day and be done with it. You have done what you could. Some blunders and absurdities no doubt crept in; forget them as soon as you can. Tomorrow is—

Suddenly, I was very sleepy.

I didn't drift off so much as dive into a deep sleep, the kind I can only experience next to Lauren.

Dreams came fast.

Not haunted, but happy.

Childhood. Good friends. Jimmy, Ernie, and Orson. Little knight errants looking for adventure. Not knowing it, but most of all looking for purpose, meaning, and love.

"I love you so much, Jimmy Riley," Lauren whispered.

And it was a grace that I woke up just enough to hear it.

ALSO BY MICHAEL LISTER

Sign up for Michael's newsletter by clicking here or go to
www.MichaelLister.com and receive a free book.

Another Quiet Night in Desparation

(The Meaning Series)

Meaning Every Moment

The Meaning of Life in Movies

Sign up for Michael's newsletter by clicking here or go to
www.MichaelLister.com and receive a free book.